BEYOND THE STORM

BEYOND THE STORM

An Acadian Odyssey

Leon Arceneaux

Writers Club Press
San Jose New York Lincoln Shanghai

Beyond The Storm
An Acadian Odyssey

Writers Club Press
an imprint of iUniverse, Inc.

For information address:
iUniverse, Inc.
5220 S. 16th St., Suite 200
Lincoln, NE 68512
www.iuniverse.com

ISBN: 0-595-21911-X

Printed in the United States of America

This book is dedicated to all the Cajuns of the world.
Wherever you may be.

This book is fictional but it is based on official documents of the time, combined with stories and legends handed down about the Exile of the Acadians. Names of persons other than Emmeline, Louis and the British officials are fictional. Any similarities to actual people are strictly coincidental. Although Emmeline LaBiche and Louis Arceneaux were real people, this is a story of what might have been. Louis Arceneaux did obtain a land grant and settle a few miles north of what is now Lafayette, Louisiana after being separated from his beloved Emmeline. An historic marker at a site called Beaubassin marks where his home once was.

PREFACE

In the year of Our Lord 1755, an entire nation was torn from its foundations. Families were separated, some never to be reunited. A nation of happy, peaceful people were made to endure untold misery and suffering. As many as half of the exiles did not survive the hardship and disease.

Because of their faith in God, their *joie de vie* (joy of life), and because they did not harbor hatred in their hearts, the Acadians flourished. From what was once a remnant, millions of Cajuns, descendents of the original Acadians, now stand proudly to attest to the courage and strength of their ancestors.

To those Acadians wrenched from their happy peaceful homeland, who brought with them unyielding faith and courage to face the future, I owe a debt of gratitude. But to the many brave souls who did not survive, I stand and salute. To these I owe a debt of honor.

CHAPTER 1

June 1755

There are times when the sky is an azure blue and the golden rays of a vibrant sun smile down on cool green meadows. These are the days when we are at peace with the world—when no evil seems to exist and we look to the future with happy expectation. But just beyond the horizon a storm may be brewing with blinding rain and clawing winds of change that can tear our tranquil world apart. And so it was with the Acadians on that June of long ago.

Louis stopped to rest as he surveyed the land he had cleared. The earthy smell of freshly plowed fields and spring meadows gave him a warm, happy, secure feeling. He wiped the sweat from his face and took a long drink from a water bag he had hung on a small tree. The water was sweet and cool.

His grandfather had been a navigator on a ship from France bringing settlers to the New World. When he stepped off of the ship, he immediately fell in love with Acadia, and stayed to marry and raise a family. He had made a wise choice. The fertile soil and friendly natives had welcomed him, and now a third generation of Arsenalts was coming into its own.

Louis poured some of the cool water on his head and let it run down his neck and face. The muscles in his arms ached but his heart was light with joy as he took a deep breath and continued his work. In September, three months away, he'll marry his lovely, Emmeline.

His father had given him the land he was clearing and his neighbors had helped him build a cabin. His friend, Fabien, had presented him with a pair of sheep as an early wedding present. There will be newborn lambs next spring, his friend had told him.

He had not yet shown Emmeline any of this. He wanted to surprise her by bringing her here after mass on Sunday. Then they'll go to his parents for dinner.

Life could not have been better, he thought, as he prepared to continue pulling up stumps where next year there will be a bountiful harvest for him and the woman he loved so dearly.

❧   ❧   ❧

Louis stood outside the church, talking with some of the other men while waiting for the LaBiche family and Emmeline.

"What's the news?" asked Pierre, Louis' father, to Etienne Boudreau. "How did the meeting go?"

Etienne had met the day before with Colonel John Winslow, the British officer in charge of the Grand Pré Area.

"We have nothing to worry about," Etienne answered. He paused, then continued. "The British wanted us to denounce our faith and pledge unconditional allegiance to the king of England…"

"What?" interrupted Pierre along with the surprised gasps of the other men. "What do you mean? We chose you to represent us!"

"Wait—wait" said Etienne impatiently. "Let me finish. Didn't I say I would look after our interests?" He slowly looked around at the faces of the men surrounding him. "Well, Colonel Winslow realized we wouldn't agree to that and there'd be trouble if he tried to force us. I told him we were citizens of Acadia. We would not pledge allegiance to either France or England."

"That's right!" someone shouted. "Yes," declared several others.

Etienne continued. "Then I reminded him that we are Neutrals and we've had neutral status since the conventions of 1730. We only want to be left alone. To live our lives in peace."

"What did he say?" Pierre asked.

"He agreed. He said that if we are truly neutral and do not cause trouble, we will be allowed to live our lives without interference," Etienne replied.

"What about our guns?" one of the men in the group asked. "Are they going to give them back to us? We need them to hunt and to protect ourselves."

"He assured me he's having discussions with the Governor. We'll be getting them back, as soon as all this settles down."

"Good," said Pierre. "I don't trust these British. They have the upper hand now that they control Acadia. But then, what can they do to us if we declare ourselves to be neutral?" There was a murmur of agreement from the other men.

"That's right," Etienne also agreed. "Yet, what else could we do? If we side with the British, then the Micmac Indians might cause us trouble. You know how they hate the British. And we have nothing to protect ourselves with."

"Yes!" one of the men shouted, "And our countrymen have abandoned us!"

Etienne continued, "But Colonel Winslow is a good man. He agreed to our neutrality. We have nothing to worry about, as long as we don't cause trouble."

"Cause trouble?" declared Pierre dropping his arms in frustration. "How could we? They have our guns."

"Well, he doesn't have to worry about trouble from us," said Louis. "All we want is to be left alone."

"Right," said one of the men gathered around Etienne. "But I'd feel much better if the British hadn't confiscated our guns. How could we have let that happen?"

"Well, one thing we do know," said Louis as he looked around for Emmeline. "We don't want to be caught in the crossfire between the British and the French." This was followed by a murmur of approval.

"Remember what Father André told us in his sermon today," Fabian said rather loudly so everyone could hear. "Love thy neighbor. That means we should love the British and pray for them. They're our brothers."

"Love them!" one of the men in the group shouted.

"What's the matter with you?" others shouted at Fabien.

"Calm down, everyone," Louis exclaimed loudly, waving his arms. "What Fabien means is we should live peaceably with them. Isn't that right, Fabian?"

"Well…" Fabian answered as all eyes were fixed on him.

"And, that's what we want to do." Louis heard Alphonse, Emmeline's brother, bellow from behind him. "If they leave us alone we'll leave them alone, but if they want trouble…"

Louis turned around on hearing Alphonse's voice. He spotted Emmeline with her family and called to her while he pushed his way through the group who had assembled around Etienne.

Alphonse put his arm around Louis' shoulder as he walked with him. "The British surprised us all when they searched our houses for guns. But we got the better of them." Alphonse ruffled Louis' hair. "You and I had our guns at our hunting camp," he said smugly. "If the Micmacs didn't find them, we still have our guns."

"Not so loud," Louis cautioned. "We can go to prison, or worse, if the British know."

"At least, you and I still have our guns," Alphonse continued in a loud whisper. "We don't know how many others still do, hidden away. If those damned British want a fight, they got it. Even if it's just you and me. Right?"

❧   ❧   ❧

"All right. Open your eyes," Louis said to Emmeline as he removed the blindfold. "What do you see?"

Emmeline was speechless.

They were on a ridge above a lush green basin or wide shallow valley. On this ridge, with a view of the land below, was a cabin made of logs.

"This is going to be our home," he continued. "Our own little corner of heaven. My father gave us the land on top of the ridge. I've been clearing it so we can farm it next year."

He took her by the hand and led her up the steps to the porch. "I saved all I made from trapping for the last three winters and bought the land down to the bottom of the basin from Felix Martin. One day I'll clear the trees on the slope and plant a vineyard. Maybe we can make our own wine and sell it." His heart was filled with pride in being able to share this moment with Emmeline.

"I'll make you a good husband," he continued as he squeezed Emmeline's hand. "You and our children will never want for anything. I promise you that. We'll call this our Beaubassin. I built the cabin looking out over the basin. On summer evenings we can sit on the porch and watch the moon come up."

"Oh, Louis!" Emmeline said softly. "I can't believe it! It's like a dream."

She threw her arms around Louis' neck and kissed him.

He held her tightly in his arms. When he held her like this, reality seemed to disappear, and it was just the two of them sealed together in their own little cocoon. But when he kissed her…when he felt her lips against his…when he tasted her breath…

She pushed him away, breathing heavily. "That's enough…stop…

Louis' heart was beating hard, pounding in his ears. He wanted to pull her back to him…to hold her tightly in his arms.

"We have to wait," the young woman said, still breathing hard. "Only three more months and then…

Only three more months, thought Louis…only! It seemed like an eternity to wait. He stood at arms length, his hands on her shoulders, taking in her beauty—dark eyes sparkling with excitement, moist red lips, loose brown curls flowing over her shoulders. He thrilled at the sight of her full firm breasts, rising and falling with each breath…the sensuous curve of her hips. He loved this woman more than he thought he could love anyone. He worked hard, just so he could make her happy. There is nothing that I wouldn't do for her, he thought.

He took a deep breath and letting it out said, "Come see what I made for us." He took her by the hand and led her to the door of the little cabin.

Louis flung the door open with a flair. After unlatching and opening the wooden shutters on the windows, light flooded into the room. In the center was a rustic table made from logs sawed in half. Next to it was a wooden bench also made from a half log. A large fireplace, with a black iron pot hanging inside, graced the far wall. The room smelled of fresh cut wood. To the right was an open doorway.

"Wait here," Louis said as he walked through the doorway into the other room and opened the wooden shutters. The room filled with the golden light of early summer.

"All right. Come in."

A bed made of hand carved and polished maple logs occupied the middle of the room. "What do you think?" he said, as he fluffed up the mattress his mother had made for them.

"Oh! It's beautiful!"

"Made the bed myself. Worked on it all winter in my spare time. It's sturdy. Able to take anything we can give it," he said, shaking the bed. "It's ready for us." Louis laughed and the young woman blushed. Her dark eyes twinkled and white teeth shown between full red lips as she smiled.

How he wished that they were already married. He longed to take her into his arms, lie in this bed and feel the soft curves of her beautiful body. Three months seemed so long to wait for paradise.

He touched her shoulder and slowly let his hand slide down her arm. Louis then took the young woman by the hand and walked out onto the porch. Two chairs made of willow branches and covered with deer hide were side by side. The hide was soft and supple. Dark brown hair, interspersed with lighter strains, lay flat and shiny. He rubbed his hand on its smooth surface. "I gave the Indians a bushel of corn to make these for us. In the evenings we can sit here and watch the moon rise."

"It's so comfortable, I could sit here for hours," she sighed.

He sat in the chair next to her. Speaking softly, he reached out and took her hand. "See that tree? That branch reaching out? I'll hang a swing from it for our children."

Emmeline squeezed his hand. "This will be a wonderful place to raise our family."

The cool, green of the tree reached out as if to embrace the little cabin and those who would venture beneath its sheltering branches. "I can't wait to sit here with you in the evenings," she mused. Louis could feel the love in her voice.

A soft breeze wafted up the slope from the valley below carrying the perfume of flowers hidden in the tangle of green. This perfume, mingled with the raw earthy smell of wild berries and dusty green leaves, awakened within the man and woman the promise of carnal delights yet to be tasted.

Reluctantly he stood, still holding her hand. "Dinner will be ready and it's a long walk to the house."

❦   ❦   ❦

Later that evening, Louis and Emmeline strolled hand in hand down the dusty lane to her house. The rays of the setting sun reflected on the dust making it look like the road was paved with gold. An owl hooted in the distance. A cool zephyr drifted across the pasture, bringing with it the fresh smell of dew and new green plants.

After a while, Emmeline broke the silence. "Your mother cooks so well," she murmured. "I wish I could cook that well. But I've been learning from my mother—you won't starve," she said with a laugh.

Louis smiled. "I don't care if your cooking tastes terrible. I'd still be happy to be married to you."

"That's what you say now," she said, tossing her curls. "You'll change your words when your stomach says, 'that's enough.'" She laughed again.

Louis loved the way she laughed. "I believe you can cook well," he said with a knowing look.

"Did I tell you my mother and I have been sewing a quilt for us?" Emmeline asked. "It's going to keep us nice and warm this winter."

Louis faked a wicked grin. "Can't wait to get under that quilt with you. I'll bet we can keep warm."

"Well, you'll just have to wait to find out how warm it gets," Emmeline said frowning. "Keep talking like that and you'll have to go see Father André for confession."

As they approached the LaBiche house, Alphonse and Emmeline's sister, Ann, walked hastily toward them.

"Ann. Alphonse." Louis greeted them.

"Damn," Alphonse muttered.

"What's the matter?" Emmeline asked.

"Ann just came back from the village. Looks like there might be trouble with the British," Alphonse answered, hitting his fist in the palm of his hand.

"What do you mean?" Louis asked.

"She said they heard that Governor Lawrence was upset with the Acadians in the District of Annapolis Royal, Mines and Pisiquid."

"Why?" asked Emmeline.

"Because..." Alphonse started, but was interrupted by Ann. "Because they refused to take the oath of allegiance. Defiant, he says. He also thinks Acadians are trying to get the Indians to up–rise against the British."

"Hope there won't be trouble in the Beausejour Region. Could spread here," Louis said almost under his breath and then added confidently, "Probably a false rumor."

I heard Colonel Moncton doesn't like Acadians," said Alphonse as he defiantly kicked the dust in the road.

Louis rubbed his face. "That's why I hope there won't be trouble in the Beausejour Region. If there's any trouble, it would definitely be in his region." He was silent for while and then continued confidently. "But then, he can't do anything to them or any other Acadians, for that matter." He patted Alphonse on the back. "We've declared ourselves Neutrals. We don't have to pledge allegiance to anyone. Governor Lawrence knows that."

"If they come here looking for trouble, they'll find out what trouble is," Alphonse boasted as he again slammed his fist into the palm of his hand. "Let 'em come."

Louis put his arm around Emmeline's waist. "Colonel Winslow is in charge of our region. Good man. Trusts us. Said we'd be left in peace..." He took a deep breath and then continued, "But I don't like to hear rumors like that. Trouble could start if people believe it."

"Well...guess you're right," Alphonse conceded. "Let the British and French fight it out. I guess as long as we stay out of politics and stay neutral..." His voice trailed off. He raised his arms then let them drop in frustration. "Hell, the French forgot about us," he continued loudly. "This is our country. We've been left alone to settle and develop it for over a hundred years. We're well entrenched here. Too many of us for the British to demand anything."

"That's right," Emmeline chided. "People are always looking for things to get excited about or have something to worry about. Louis and I are going to get married, have a nice farm, raise a family and be happy. And no one is going to change that."

Louis looked at Emmeline and smiled. "Yes. No one is going to change that." He faced Alphonse and continued. "It took a lot of years to develop what we have here and make it into a land any country would be proud of. We know how to work this land and make it productive. The British don't want to lose that." He turned back to Emmeline and kissed her on the forehead.

"Enough of that," Alphonse said as he playfully slapped Louis on the back.

"Leave them alone," scolded Ann.

Louis ran his fingers through Emmeline's hair. "The British won't do anything," he said confidently. "We have nothing to worry about." Still, deep down in his heart, he did not feel as confident as he sounded.

CHAPTER 2

August, 1755

Colonel John Winslow sat at his desk as he wrote in his journal. His wife walked up behind him and looked over his shoulder.

"Do you think we'll have trouble with the Acadians?" she asked as she rubbed the back of his neck.

"Read what I've written," he said as he handed her his journal.

She read it aloud. "We are now hatching the great and noble project of banishing the French Neutrals from the Province."

"But," she said as she handed back the small, black book. "I thought you told the Acadians that you would not bother them as long as they remained neutral?"

"Which would you rather have in this province," the colonel answered, "Frenchmen or good British farmers? There are many good, hard working Puritan farmers looking for the Promised Land. They can move into these farms that will be waiting for them.

"And which would you rather have here, Frenchmen that you can't understand or good, honest, hard working, Christian, British citizens whom you can understand and trust?"

"I guess you're right…But you told them differently. How are you going to make them leave?" the lady said almost in a whisper as she ran her fingers along the braided hair hanging from the back of his head. "Will we be in danger?"

"Governor Lawrence broached the idea of deportation when he was in London last year. It was received quite well," the colonel said as he puffed on his pipe. "So, when Lawrence returned from London, he asked Judge Morris, the Provincial Surveyor, to prepare a report on how to go about banishing them."

"But will we be in danger?" the lady repeated worriedly.

The colonel stood up, turned around and kissed his wife on the forehead. "There's nothing to worry about," he said reassuringly. "Remember, we confiscated their firearms and Governor William Shirley of Massachusetts promised enough ships to carry away all of the Acadians." The colonel puffed on his pipe and grinned smugly. "And remember, this is no longer Acadia. It is New Scotland, Nova Scotia. We can't have Frenchmen living in New Scotland now, can we?"

"Well...no," she said hesitantly. "But it just doesn't seem right to take their land."

"But darling, it is right," the colonel responded. "It's not their land. It now belongs to the British Crown."

"What will happen to them? Will they ever be a danger to us?" his wife asked as she looked up into her husband's eyes.

The colonel smiled. "Don't worry. They'll be scattered so that they will never be able to come together again. Besides, when this great and noble project is completed, I am sure that the Crown will reward us handsomely.

"The plan is already underway," he continued. "Here, read this copy of the instructions that Lawrence has sent to me; to Robert Moncton, the Commanding Officer of the Beausejour Region; Captain John Handfield, Commander of Annapolis Royal; and Alexander Murry of Pisiquid. He also sent his intentions to the board of trade in London. So, you see, there's no stopping it now." He smiled again as he handed the papers to his wife to read.

She read the words out loud in a hushed tone: "The Acadians have refused to take the oath of allegiance and it is determined that they be removed out of the country as soon as possible. For this purpose, a sufficient number of transports will be sent up for taking them on board." She stopped, took a deep breath, and slowly let it out in a sigh.

She continued: "It is necessary to keep this a secret to prevent any attempt to escape and the carrying off of their cattle. Their land, cattle and crops are forfeited to the Crown for the expense the government will incur in transporting them out of the country. The inhabitants now have no property in their name. They will be allowed to take only their ready money and what they can carry." She stopped again as if to absorb the significance of what she had just read. She wet her lips and again continued reading but her voice was now low and subdued, almost a whisper.

"You are instructed to detain the men, both young and old, into your power so the women and children will not be able to carry off the cattle."

The woman finished reading the instructions, slowly folded the paper and silently handed it to her husband. A tear rolled down her cheek.

"We're doing this for the Crown," the colonel said softly, looking into her eyes and wiping the tear from her cheek with his thumb. "War is like that. It can't be helped. People get hurt. If it would be the other way around, they would do the same to us."

As she turned to walk away, the Colonel's wife said in barely a whisper, "Would they?"

CHAPTER 3

September 4, 1755

The village of Grand Pré was celebrating a successful harvest. The hope of every farmer in the area was more than fulfilled. There would be enough to supply all of their needs for the coming winter with plenty to sell to the British. Louis mulled this over in his mind as he approached the town square. Maybe now the British will see the value of the Acadian Neutrals. The shopkeepers also had reason to celebrate, as there would be an abundance of hard money available for the farmers to use.

Louis could hear the music of the accordion and fiddles coming from the Town Square. Calves and pigs had been donated for slaughter, and food was being prepared for everyone.

He was in a festive mood. Not only was he here to celebrate with his neighbors, but in three more days he would marry Emmeline. She would be here with her family.

"Hey, brother–in–law!"

Louis saw Alphonse approaching. "Not so fast. I won't be your brother–in–law for three more days."

Alphonse roughed up Louis' hair. "Close enough to call you that. Emmeline has really been preparing. She has her wedding dress finished. One of girls is going to sing. Songs are all picked out and she's been practicing at our house. I'm about to go crazy with all that singing over and over. They also made sure Father André would be prepared and waiting. Poor man, they've been pestering him with the scripture readings, the songs and everything."

They walked toward the sound of the music and festivities. Alphonse had his arm around Louis' shoulders.

Louis laughed. "I'm sure glad the only thing the groom has to do is be there," he commented.

"You better be there," Alphonse said as he tightened his grip on Louis' neck with the crook of his arm.

"I wouldn't miss it for the world," Louis laughed.

"Well, brother–in–law, let's go get some of that cider my father brought. It's good and strong. From last year," Alphonse said.

They toasted the harvest and the two men drank a cup of the cider.

Ann ran up to Louis. "Let's dance," she said.

"Where's Emmeline?" Louis asked.

"She's around," Ann answered. "But right now I want to dance with my soon to be brother–in–law."

Ann smiled as she danced with Louis. "I'm so glad you're marrying my sister. I know you'll make her happy. Momma and Poppa said they could not have picked out a better man for Emmeline."

"Thank you," Louis said, a little embarrassed. "I'm glad your family feels that way about me. I love Emmeline and want to make her happy." He looked over Ann's shoulder. "Here she comes now."

"Little sister," Emmeline said, faking a scold. "You're keeping my man from me."

"He's all yours," Ann said with a laugh. "He said he wants to make you happy. Can you make him happy?"

Emmeline looked at Louis and smiled. "Oh, yes. In three more days, I'll make him very happy."

Louis took Emmeline in his arms and started dancing. "I love you," he whispered in her ear. He pushed back her hair and kissed her neck.

The music stopped and on the cool autumn air Louis smelled the rich aroma of meat cooking on an open fire. Its juices landing on burning coals sent its savory smoke wafting on the breezes.

The smell made Louis feel a twinge of hunger. "Let's get something to eat while the musicians are resting." He took Emmeline by the hand and led her to where the smells were coming from.

"Hey, Jock," Louis said as he approached a friend who was preparing the meat. "Smells good."

Jock didn't answer. He was looking past them.

Louis noticed a strange hush in the excited talk around him. "What's going on?" he muttered.

"Everyone! Let me have your attention!"

At the sound of the words, Louis turned toward the makeshift stage where the musicians had been playing. On the stage were two British soldiers with guns and bayonets drawn, on either side of an officer. One of the soldiers fired his musket into the air. There was a deathly silence.

The officer stepped forward. "Everyone listen to me," he shouted in French. "I have a proclamation from Colonel John Winslow, British officer in charge of the Grand Pré Region."

He unrolled a scroll and started reading.

"I, John Winslow, acting under the order of Governor Lawrence, in the name of the British Crown, do hereby order all men and boys over the age of ten years to gather in the church tomorrow morning, one hour after sunrise, there to hear His Majesty's intentions. Anyone who does not show up will forfeit his land and cattle."

The officer rolled up the scroll. "It is up to you to advise anyone who is not here to be in the church tomorrow morning." He solemnly left the stage flanked by the two solders. There was a stunned silence and then a low murmur.

Etienne Boudreau climbed up on the stage. "Listen to me!" he shouted. "Do not panic. We are to gather to hear His Majesty's intention, that's all. He probably sent word that being Neutrals, we will be allowed to live in peace. Do not risk trouble by not showing up. Show some respect to the British crown and we will prove our neutrality. I'll be there tomorrow to look after your interest." He waived his arms over his head. "Let's not let this dampen our celebration. Colonel Winslow is a good man. He will not cause us trouble. Play the music! Dance! Eat!"

The music started again, but the air was not as festive as before.

"Do you want to go home?" Louis said to Emmeline. "I just don't have a good feeling about all this. I don't know what the British king's intentions are, but remember we're French and he's English."

He took her by the hand, and then as if to belay her fears, he continued, "But then, again, we're Acadians and we're not at war with him."

When they reached Emmeline's house, they lingered in the moonlight.

"Emmeline," Louis said as he kissed her fingertips. "As I was saying, I don't know what the king's intentions are, but no matter what happens, we'll be together. We'll give each other love and happiness for the rest of our lives. Nobody can stop that. We'll always find a way."

He held her face in his hands and continued, "After we hear the king's intentions, I'll come back here and tell you about it. Even if the king puts a tax on us, we'll still have our own little corner of heaven. Our Beaubassin."

Louis pulled the young woman close to him. He put his face in her soft curls, smelling her fragrance. Then he held her tightly and they kissed—a long, lingering kiss.

"Good night," he whispered as he kissed her again. "Sleep well. Don't think about the British. Dream good dreams. Dream about our future at Beaubassin. Just a few short days away."

He turned to walk away, but after a few steps, stopped to look back at her one more time. Moonlight sparkled in her hair as her curls fell softly around her shoulders. The pale silver of the harvest moon caressed her face. She smiled. He etched this picture in his mind. Then he heard her voice—soft and sweet as a summer breeze—words that he would remember when the storm clouds gather. "Good night, my love. Remember, beyond the storm, the sun still shines."

Louis, his father Pierre and his younger brother Jean, put on their jackets as they prepared to leave for the meeting at the church. Louis kissed his mother and sister Marie. "Don't worry, everything will be fine," he said, although he didn't feel that way. Deep down in his heart he felt that something was wrong. Even with all the reassurances, something did not seem right. Things just didn't add up.

As they walked toward the church, Louis asked his father, "Why did they threaten to confiscate our property if we didn't attend?"

"I don't know," his father replied. He was silent for a while thinking, then continued. "Etienne talked with Winslow and he assured him that no harm would come to us. But can we really trust the British?"

"Well, whether we do or not, what difference will it make?" Jean commented.

"Yes," Louis said as he raised the collar of his jacket against a cold wind that had begun to blow. "What difference does it make? There's not much we can do about it." The sunrise cast a pink glow on the frost that covered the fields. The dust on the road swirled in the air with each gust of wind. "The British have the upper hand," he continued. "They can force us to do anything they want us to do. Could even force us to hand over all our surplus crops to their army without any payment. But we'd survive. There's always next year."

"Well, I'm getting to be an old man," said his father. "Don't have time left for many setbacks."

"You're not old," Jean said. "There's many more harvests left in you. And remember you have us. We'll always be here to help you with the harvest."

As they neared the church, other men joined them, each with a differing opinion on what the king's intentions were.

Upon seeing Alphonse, Louis shouted a greeting. Alphonse responded loudly. "Don't worry, we're meeting in the church. Nothing bad will happen in God's holy place. Besides, Father André will be there."

The men slowly filed through the doors. Friends and acquaintances greeted each other, but there were no smiles. Silently they sat in the pews nervously shuffling their feet. Some knelt and crossed themselves in prayer. Others stood solemnly in the isles.

In the silence of the church, fear crept into the minds of the anxious men. Fear of the unknown intentions of their adversaries. Although they would not admit it to each other, they knew that this must be a moment of serious consequences.

After all of the men had assembled, a roll call was made based on the British census. When it was assured that all of the men were there, except for the ones too sick to come, (the roll showed 418 men were present), the doors of the church were slammed shut and locked.

A cry rose from the men—a cry of anger, fear and betrayal. Some rushed toward the doors, but the doors were solid oak and they held. A call went up for Father André.

The priest walked slowly onto the altar, his head down, a British soldier with drawn bayonet on either side. There was silence to hear what he had to say.

"My fellow Acadians, we have been betrayed."

As soon as the words left the priest's mouth, one of the soldiers slapped his face. Some of the men started toward the altar but they were met by the points of bayonets as five more soldiers rushed in from the sacristy.

The priest put his hand on his face, then looked intently at the men held prisoner in his church.

"My children." He stood silently for a moment, then continued. "Listen to what Colonel Winslow has to say. But I stand before God and condemn the evil that is upon us today. Whatever happens, stand strong and do not denounce your faith."

When he finished speaking, one of the soldiers cried out, "Papist!" and struck him with the butt of his gun. The priest staggered and fell to his knees. A gasp rose from the throats of all the men and boys assembled. Some of the boys started crying softly.

Colonel Winslow strode onto the altar and was met with cries of anger. He chastised the soldier for striking Father André and instructed the soldiers to help the priest to the rectory. When the soldiers left, Winslow held up his hand for silence.

"I apologize for my soldiers actions to your priest."

A roar of outrage from the assembled men met his words.

Winslow again held up his hand. He waited, then spoke. "The soldier had no right to strike your priest. I promise you that he will be punished." He hesitated, looked out over the sea of angry faces, took a deep breath, let it out with a sigh and then continued. "I have received orders from the Governor to place all of you under arrest."

There was a shocked silence.

Etienne spoke up. "Why? We are Neutrals. On what charges are you arresting us?"

"Ah, my friend," the Colonel answered. "I can only do what I am ordered to do. As the British officer in charge of Grand Pré, I have been instructed by Governor Lawrence to issue this order, which I shall read to you."

He broke the seal on a folded paper and read the order:

"Your lands and tenants, cattle of all kinds and livestock of all sorts are forfeited to the Crown with all your other effects save your ready money and household goods, and you yourselves will be removed from this Province. That it is His Majesty's orders that the whole French inhabitants of these Districts be removed. I am, through His Majesty's goodness, directed to allow you the liberty to carry your money and bring with you whatever household goods you can without overloading the vessel you go in." He stopped, looked up, took a deep breath, then continued reading the order: "I shall do everything in my power that these goods be secured to you and that you are not molested in carrying of them, and also that whole families shall go in the same vessel. I shall make this remove, which I am sure gives you a great deal of trouble, as easy as His Majesty's service will allow. I hope that in which ever part of the world you may fall, you may be faithful subjects, a peaceable and happy people." He was silent, then in a voice that was hardly audible, continued, "Signed…Governor Lawrence."

The Colonel slowly folded the paper, his hand visibly trembling, and strode off of the altar, into the sacristy and out of the church. The door was slammed shut and bolted.

There was again a shocked silence. The men looked at each other in confused disbelief. Muffled words flowed from their lips—questions without answers. "What does this mean? How can this be? How will they do it? What will happen to us?"

Louis was numb. He couldn't believe what he had just witnessed and heard. Although he had been apprehensive, he didn't think that it would be this drastic.

"Will they actually take us away?" Louis kept repeating the question to himself.

Alphonse came up to Louis. "Don't worry, brother–in–law. They won't ship us out. The British don't have enough ships to transport all of us. They're bluffing. They'll let us out in time for your wedding."

Someone opened a stained glass window to let fresh air in. "Dear God have mercy! *Mon Dieu!* The harbor!" A shout echoed and reverberated within the closed confines of the church. "The harbor!" It echoed off the walls where paintings depicted the way of the cross.

The cry echoed around a life–sized crucifix behind the altar where a statue of Jesus—blood running down his face from a crown of thorns—looked down at this pitiful, confused and frightened humanity.

At the sound of the cry, Louis ran toward the window. Fear and apprehension swirled around him like a cold fog. His heart pounded in his chest. Maybe he was having a nightmare and would wake up. He blinked hard and looked again. From the window he could see the harbor. Panic and fear became real and clutched at his very soul. The harbor was filled with ships, their tall masts rocking with the waves. "No!" he choked. "No…this can't be happening! Dear God! Don't let this be happening!"

That night, the colonel wrote in his journal: "They were greatly struck. Although I believe they did not imagine that they would actually be removed. Thus ended the memorable 5th of September, a day of great fatigue and trouble."

CHAPTER 4

"*E*verybody outside!"

As the doors of the church were flung open, the golden morning sun flooded through the portal. Where before, this golden flood once held a warm promise of the coming day, it now held a hollow meaning, like the coins that once glistened in the hands of a man named Judas.

Louis rubbed his eyes and sat up. He ached from sleeping on the hard floor. He had to curl up in the fetal position to be able to find a place to sleep. Some had slept on the pews while he and others slept underneath. Old men groaned as they tried to sit up while their tired bones cried out to them in pain. Young boys, who had cried themselves to sleep, sobbed, as they realized that this wasn't a nightmare and was really true. Then there were the curses by the young men that were hurled at their captors.

Slowly, the men moved from the church into the churchyard. The stale smell of unwashed bodies mixed with the smell of urine was left behind in the church. Louis walked into the early morning light and took a deep breath of fresh air.

"Where's our father?" Louis asked Jean.

"He's coming, but he's a little slow this morning. I think he's talking to one of his friends. Some of them think the British might let us go home today."

"Wishful thinking...the ships in the bay. Why do you think they're here?" Louis said tiredly. "Look at the soldiers. If we were going home they wouldn't need all those soldiers. No, little brother, they just won't accept reality."

After everyone was out of the church, a British officer stood on the church steps and spoke to the men in French. "You are surrounded by soldiers. They have orders to shoot anyone who tries to escape. Remember you are all under arrest by order of the Crown."

Some of the men milled around talking to each other in low tones. Others sat on the ground. Reality was slowly starting to sink in to those who had not accepted it before. The quietness which now descended upon this pitiful group was the quietness of a condemned man who finally realizes that there is no way to escape his fate...that his fate is real and final.

"I wonder what's going to happen next?" Louis spoke to Jean almost unbelievingly. "What's going to happen to our families? What about our mother and Marie? What about Emmeline? Tomorrow was our wedding day!" Louis fought a lump in his throat as he thought of Emmeline. He longed to hold her face in his hands and kiss her soft lips. He could smell the fragrance of her hair and skin.

A wagon drew up and two British soldiers held up loaves of bread for the men to see. The men filed slowly toward the wagon. Louis didn't feel hungry but he thought he had better eat to keep his strength.

"Get our father," Louis told Jean. "We need to make sure he gets something to eat."

Each man was given half a loaf of bread and a dipper of water to drink. The bread was fresh and the water was cool.

"Look down the road!" someone yelled.

A river of humanity was approaching. As they got closer, Louis saw women carrying babies and young children. Some were pulling carts loaded with their possessions and sick or crippled parents. When they saw the men, a wail rose from their throats. "They're burning our houses!"

Louis now saw columns of smoke in the distance where farm-houses were. He heard screams as houses and shops in the town were put to the torch. His heart beat fast. His mouth was dry and he broke out in a cold sweat. *Dear God! What are they doing?*

He saw his mother and Marie pulling a loaded cart. His mother called out to her husband. "Pierre! They burned our house and shot our dogs! This is all we have left." She let out a heart–rending wail.

Louis and Jean started toward her. British soldiers with fixed bayonets stopped them. The soldiers made signs to the women to keep moving. Pierre shouted after his wife and daughter, "Don't worry! We'll soon be together! I'll take care of you! Everything will be all right!"

"We love you, Mama," Louis called after them. "We love you." He saw Marie stumble and almost fall as she helped her mother with the cart. She was crying. He heard Jean sob and put his arm around him.

Louis looked around for his father who stood motionless, visibly shaken. "It's going to be all right, Papa," he said. "It's going to be all right when we all get together again." Louis mouthed the words but he really didn't believe what he was saying.

Women, children and babies screamed and cried. Louis felt helpless. He wanted to run out and stop this insanity. This couldn't really be happening…it couldn't!

"Where are they making them go?" Jean asked Louis.

Louis couldn't answer at first, there was such a lump in his throat. "Looks like they're taking them to the Town Square."

"Louis!" A voice cried out.

Louis turned to see Emmeline helping her mother pull a cart piled high.

"Louis! They burned our house. They also burned the house you built for us!" Emmeline cried out between sobs.

"No!" Louis screamed. "They can't."

"I still have my wedding dress…" Emmeline looked back over her shoulder as the soldiers shoved her forward. "Remember beyond the storm…the sun…" A soldier pushed her to make her hurry and she fell to her knees.

"Emmeline!" Louis shouted. He tried to push past the soldiers to get to Emmeline…to touch her…but a soldier shoved him back and he fell. He struggled to his feet and screamed after her, "I love you! I love you!" His breath came in short gasps and his heart raced in his chest. Why are they doing this to us, he thought. We haven't done anything to deserve this. We just want to live our lives in peace. Why won't they let us? All I want to do is to marry my Emmeline and raise a family.

Anger surged through him like a red–hot sword. "Damn you! Damn you! Damn you!" Louis shouted at the soldiers. His shouts ended in painful sobs. Other men heard Louis' shout and they too started shouting. The soldiers turned to face the men gathered in the churchyard and pointed their bayonets at them. The shouting subsided into low cursing.

Louis' father put his arm around him. "Don't worry, son. Everything will turn out all right. We'll come back when France wins the next war with England."

"When will that be?" Louis asked. "How many years will we have to wait? If we hadn't been forced into giving up our guns, we would have outnumbered the British troops. They wouldn't have been able to do this to us." He breathed deeply trying to keep from sobbing. "It's too late. There's nothing to come back to. It's all over."

"I don't know where they're sending us, but we can come together with arms and take back our land," said Jean.

"Yes," Alphonse joined in. "Even though we didn't have a chance to get to our guns, France will give us arms. We have the British outnumbered. They don't know it, but they've already spelled their doom."

"Let's not do anything rash," said Pierre. "We don't want any bloodshed. The king of England will realize his mistake and return us to our homes. We'll have to rebuild, but we can do it. We're a strong people. If we all stick together we can do it."

"What have they done to our lives?" said Louis. "We can't ever be like we were before. What can we do?" He couldn't understand how anyone could be so evil as to destroy the lives of an entire people. His life with Emmeline was shattered. A helpless hatred wrenched and tore at his soul. There was nothing that he could do to stop this evil. "What can we do?" he repeated.

"What can we do, brother–in–law?" said Alphonse. "What can we do? We can fight back! We can destroy them like they're trying to destroy us!"

"Louis," a familiar voice said. "I can't believe this is happening."

Louis turned around as Fabien walked slowly toward him, head down, shuffling his feet.

"Fabien. I didn't see you in the church. Where were you?"

"I'm so sorry, Louis. I heard they burned the cabin we helped you build and shot your dog."

At hearing the words, Louis felt cold shock flood over him again. "Are you sure?" he asked, looking directly into Fabien's eyes. "They shot my dog, too?"

Fabien hugged Louis. "Yes, I'm sure. They took the two sheep I gave you. They took everybody's livestock. My mama told me as she went by. She saw."

Stepping back, Fabien looked around him. "They took every-thing…to pay the King of England." He said loudly and sarcastically. "For what? To ship us out from our homeland?" He spit as if to get a nasty taste out of his mouth.

"To pay the king?" Louis asked. How do you know?"

"A soldier told me."

One of the men approached Fabien with a sneer, "Are you still praying for our brothers, the British?"

Fabien didn't answer.

The last of the women and children finally passed as they were herded onto the Town Square.

"Attention!" a British officer bellowed in French.

A hush fell over the men in the churchyard.

"Attention! You men will be escorted to the ships. You will board the ships as you arrive."

"No!" The men shouted as one and rushed toward the soldiers. They were stopped by the points of bayonets. A wail went out from the throats of the Acadian men. "What about our families?"

"The men will board first," the officer replied.

"What about our clothes and personal effects?" someone yelled.

"The women have the personal effects," the officer said.

"Where are we going?" someone else asked.

"You'll find out when you get there."

British soldiers lined both sides of the street with drawn bayonets.

The officer bellowed out in French again. "Go in single file and stop at the docks. I will say who goes into each ship."

As the men filed down the street, they could hear the women screaming after them. Louis' heart broke when he heard the cries and wails of the women as he shuffled by. Some were on their knees praying, others were singing religious hymns.

When the first man arrived at the dock, the line stopped. The British officer counted the first group of men and gave an order to one of the soldiers. The soldier stepped forward and put his bayonet behind the last man that the officer pointed to who happened to be Louis' father.

"Wait, that's my father!" yelled Louis. "We're together! We're family!" The soldier turned his bayonet toward Louis.

When that group had boarded their ship, Louis was directed to wade to the longboats that would take them to the next ship. Some of the men were forced to man the oars.

Louis watched the distance widen between him and the shore. Would they ever be able to return? The cold, clammy wind went through his jacket as the waves hit the side of the boat and the spray dripped from his face. The boat hit the side of the ship with a bang.

Hesitantly, the men slowly climbed the rope ladder from the long-boat up onto the ship's deck. Old men had to be helped by the younger men as they slowly and painfully pulled themselves up.

One man with long white hair and a flowing white beard, groaned as he tried to navigate the rope ladder. Half way up he stopped, and with a cry of pain, let go. A young man below tried to hold him but lost his grip. The old man fell, bounced off of the side of the long-boat and disappeared beneath the water. One of the Acadians in the longboat dove into the water after him. There was a loud gunshot. When the smoke cleared, there were only bloody bubbles to mark the spot.

They were shoved and herded into the dark hole below the deck of the ship. Louis felt sick. As the darkness closed around them, he was filled with fear and dread. It was as if some huge monster had swallowed them. Would they become part of this sickening void or would they be vomited up into some unknown world? What was their fate? Was it so easy for the British to kill…to destroy them? It took a while for Louis' eyes to get used to the faint light from the opening to the deck. He looked around him. "Jean, Alphonse, Fabien. Are you here?"

"Yes," he heard replies from all three.

"Our father's on another ship." The words stumbled weakly from Jean's mouth.

"Yes, I know." "We'll find him when the ship docks."

"We'll come back," said Alphonse. "When we come back, we'll have guns."

"Not so loud," cautioned Louis. "Don't let them hear that. They might shoot you too. They might kill us all."

"When they fool with me," Alphonse replied, "They're asking for trouble. And they'll get it, believe me."

Louis needed to hear something positive, even if it was just Alphonse's bragging. Maybe there was a chance to return. He was ready to grasp at even the tiniest spark of hope. Right now there was only confusion and uncertainty.

"I'm scared," said Fabien, almost in a whisper. "What do you think they'll do to us?" He grabbed Louis' arm in a viselike grip. "I know I'm supposed to have faith and trust in God…but it's hard to do when you're scared. Is that wrong?"

"Just relax, and don't worry," Louis told Fabien. "Have faith. Everything will be all right. We'll gather together after we get to where we're going and decide what to do." He struggled to make his words sound as if he really believed what he was saying, but deep down in his heart the future was a dark, impenetrable fog. Where was God? Had he forgotten us, or was he somewhere in that dark suffocating fog. Have faith, he kept telling himself. God will find us. But did God even know where we were?

Colonel Winslow had watched as the women and children slowly and sadly stumbled past him. The smoke from the burning buildings had turned a bright blue autumn day into dark oppression. Not wanting to watch any longer, he had closed the blinds on his office.

"It's out of my hands," he mumbled under his breath. "Now that Governor Lawrence has sent Colonel Moncton to expedite the removal of these people, it's out of my hands." He poured himself some brandy, took a swallow and sat at his desk. "It's out of my hands," he repeated to himself.

The order that Colonel Moncton had brought with him lay on the desk. Colonel Winslow read the words softly, under his breath.

"Detain the men, both young and old into your power so as to be ready to be shipped off, as soon as the boats arrive. Then ship the women and children afterwards to different destinations far from each other." Crumpling the paper in his hand, he threw it on the floor and gulped down another swallow of brandy.

He didn't see the men being separated from their families and herded onto the ships. He didn't see soldiers taking the meager possessions from the women. He didn't hear the anguished cries of mothers being separated from their children.

The colonel made an entry in his journal: "The inhabitants, sadly and with great sorrow, abandoned their homes. The women, in great distress, carried their newborn or their youngest children in their arms. Others pulled carts with their household effects and crippled parents. It was a scene of confusion, despair, and desolation."

.

CHAPTER 5

*I*n the half–light from the opened deck hatch, Louis looked around him. A pitiful group. He estimated that there were about one hundred and fifty men and boys in the hole of the ship. They were so crowded that they could not all sleep at one time. Those who were able to climb the ladder out of the hole were allowed to go on deck, a few at a time, squint at the bright sunlight twice a day, eat some moldy bread, drink a swallow of water and return. Short respites from the stale stench of unwashed bodies, vomit and body waste.

On the third day out, Louis couldn't stand it any longer. He had to find out where they were going and what was happening to their families. "Is there anyone who can speak English?" he cried over the creaks and groans of the ship and the waves crashing against the bow.

"I can," someone in the semi–darkness of the hole spoke up.

"Come over here," Louis said. "Who are you?"

"I'm Joseph, the shop keeper." A white haired man pushed through the group. "I learned English by selling to the British in the village."

"Yes, I know you," Louis said. "Joseph, you can be a lot of help to us. First we need to find out where they're taking us and where our families will be. The next time we go on deck for our rations, ask someone. They should know and tell us."

The next day, after the rations were given out, Louis got Joseph aside. "What did you find out?"

"We're going to Charles Towne in Carolina," Joseph answered.

Alphonse heard Joseph and asked, "What about our families? Are they going to Carolina, too?"

"They said they don't know," Joseph answered, scratching his head.

"I haven't seen any other ships when we were up on deck," Louis said.

"Those bastards!" Alphonse hissed through his teeth. "We have to find our families! There are more of us than them. We can take over the ship, turn it around and find our families."

"No," Louis countered. "Some of us will get killed, and if we lose they'll kill all of us. Wait 'till we get to Carolina. We'll go back. We'll find out where our families are. I'll find Emmeline."

"What are we going to do?" Fabien asked, rubbing his hands together. "I want to get back with my family. My father's on one ship and my mother and sisters are on another. I'm afraid they'll put us in prison. They might even execute us."

"Be a man!" Alphonse sternly reprimanded Fabien. "We're going to fight to get our land back, but we only want men, not cowards."

"Alphonse!" Louis raised his voice. "We're all brothers! We have to support each other! This is hard on all of us! If we stick together and support each other, we'll get through this. If we don't, we won't make it."

"Well…maybe you're right, brother–in–law," Alphonse answered hesitantly. He was quiet for a moment then said loudly, "We'll stick together and destroy those bastards!"

Someone nearby heard Alphonse's cry and picked up the tone of the moment by crying, "Yes, we'll destroy those British bastards! British bastards!"

Others echoed the cry, and soon the ship was resounding with the cries of, "British bastards!" Louis was afraid that the situation might get out of hand and the men might try to rush the crew who were armed.

The crack of a pistol shot echoed in the confined space. A crew-member hollered something in English through the opened hatch. The frenzy subsided.

"Be careful, Alphonse," Louis said. "It doesn't take much to get this group started. We can lead them, but it must be the right time."

"We'll get these bastards, won't we, brother–in–law?" Alphonse said as he caught Louis' neck in the crook of his arm and squeezed playfully. "You're still going to marry my sister. We're going to find them soon."

Emmeline…Louis wondered. Where could she be? I'll find her, he promised himself. I'll find her. They would have been married by now and living in their own little cabin surrounded by love if it hadn't been for the British. What had he ever done to make them do this to him? Why did they hate him? All he ever wanted was to live in peace. A sob welled up in his throat, but he took a deep breath and held it back and in its place, anger and thirst for revenge gripped his soul with its iron claws.

The days and weeks passed and the group of men became more and more discouraged and weak from hunger. Each day bodies were dragged up the ladder and brought up on the deck where the ship's crew tossed them into the rolling sea. The old and the sickly suc-cumbed to the stale air, and body waste in the bottom of the ship. Silence, broken only now and then by the groans of the dying, per-meated the group of lost souls in the gloom of the ship's belly. If words were spoken, they were in hushed tones as men awakening from a nightmare.

"Louis," Jean whispered. "How are we going to find our family?"

"I don't know," Louis replied. "I really don't know. Once we get off this ship, we can regroup and decide what to do."

"We need to go back, so we can find out where they sent them," Alphonse said.

"How will we do that?" Louis asked halfheartedly. But then determination filled him as he thought of Emmeline. "Damn! We will do it! I'll make them pay for what they've done."

"Yes," Alphonse grunted. "It's the only way. Somehow we'll get guns and take our country back from those bastards. We'll find out where they sent our families and bring them home."

One morning the men were awakened by activity on the deck. From the loud talk and dragging of ropes, Louis knew that they were docking. Finally one of the sailors stuck his head in the hole and yelled something in English.

Alphonse, who had been sleeping, sat up. "What did he say?"

Louis looked at Joseph.

"This is where we're going. Everyone is to get off of the ship." Joseph answered nervously.

"Fabien! Jean! Wake up! This is where we get off this tub!" Alphonse yelled.

Louis and Alphonse led the group as they filed off the ship and onto the dock—a ragtag group of disoriented, discouraged men and boys, fearful of what may lie ahead. They had only the clothes on their backs and what they had carried in their pockets. Louis looked around him at the sad lot. Only about a hundred had survived of the one hundred and fifty who had begun the ordeal. A crowd of curious townspeople quickly formed.

"Let's go into the town and find out where we are," Alphonse said. "Maybe they'll give us something to eat."

"Wait," said Louis.

A finely dressed man came forward and said something in English.

"You be the interpreter," Louis told Joseph. "Ask him who he is and find out where we are."

"He said that he is the mayor. We are in Carolina…in Charles Town. He wants to know who we are and why we are here," said Joseph.

"Tell him we are Acadian Neutrals and the British have made us leave our country," said Louis.

"The mayor wants to know if we are prisoners," said Joseph.

"We are not prisoners. We only want to stay here until we decide what we will do. Tell him that," said Louis.

Joseph looked downhearted.

"What did he say?" asked Louis.

"We can't stay here. We must leave," Joseph said softly.

"Where can we go?" Louis asked.

"Let's storm the ship and take it." Alphonse said. "We have enough people to do it."

"Our men are too weak and the ship's crew has guns and swords," Louis countered. "Besides, we would have to also fight the townspeople from behind us. Too many of us would get slaughtered, especially the old men and the boys."

"Maybe we could surprise them and take the ship when they're not expecting us," said Jean.

"They're watching us too closely," replied Louis.

"Why don't we surrender and let the townspeople take us prisoner," said Fabien. "After they find out who we are, maybe they'll help us."

"They don't want us," Louis said.

"What do we do?" Joseph asked Louis.

"Put it to the mayor. Ask him what are we to do?"

After a consultation with the mayor, Joseph returned and spoke with Louis. "We're to stay here while he meets with the town officials. In the meantime, they'll send food and drink for us if we don't cause trouble."

"All right, everyone," Alphonse spoke loudly so as to be heard by the group of Acadians. "Be calm. We will have food and drink while we wait for them to decide what to do."

Fabien spoke softly into Louis' ear. "Suppose they decide to get rid of us by killing us."

"Don't worry, Fabien," Louis said as he put his arm around Fabien's shoulders. "We'll get through this all right. If they wanted to kill us, they wouldn't feed us."

"What's Fabien saying now?" Alphonse asked impatiently.

"He's worried. We're all worried," Louis answered.

"Well, I'm not worried," said Alphonse with much bravado. "Let 'em bring it on. We can handle anything they can hand out."

"Let's keep low until we find out what they're going to do," cautioned Louis. "Besides, our group is too weak to do anything. We need food and fresh air."

After the townspeople brought the Acadians food and drink, the Mayor came forward with a group of officials. Joseph conferred with them, then returned to Louis smiling.

"The townspeople have two boats that could accommodate our group. They will give them to us and they will give us provisions and permit us go wherever we wish."

"These are good people," Alphonse said. "We won't have to fight 'em."

"This seems too good to be true," Louis commented in a low voice. "Why are they doing this for us? What are they up to?"

"Maybe they feel sorry for us," said Jean.

Governor Lawrence looked at the official letter from the Board of Trade in London. He broke the seal and opened it.

The letter read: "The board has received the notice of your intentions. We have just concluded delicate negotiations with France. We have promised France that there is no intention to force the Acadians from Nova Scotia.

"It cannot be too much recommended to you to use the greatest caution and prudence in your conduct toward these Neutrals, and to assure such of them, as may be trusted, especially upon their taking the Oaths to his Majesty, that they may remain in quiet possession of their settlements, under proper regulations."

The letter was signed, Sir Thomas Robinson, Member of Board of Trade.

Governor Lawrence turned pale and with shaking hands read the letter again.

"Too late," he said under his breath. "Too late."

He took a lighted candle from his desk and held it to the letter. The flame consumed all but the corner that he held in his hand, then he let the burning corner drift to the floor and ground the ashes with his foot.

"I've done a good job for His Majesty and for my country. They will never be able to ever return. History will prove that I am right."

CHAPTER 6

*L*ouis looked at the two sad looking boats and the moldy bread and wormy corn on the dock. The ship that had taken them had already departed. He took a deep breath. These people are not doing us a favor. They're getting rid of us, their rotten food and their rotten boats all at one time. But we can't stay here, he thought. He looked around him at the group of men and boys anxiously wanting to leave. We don't know how sea worthy these boats are. He heaved a sigh. What else can we do?

"Well, these bastards are not any better than the rest," Alphonse sneered. "But maybe we can keep these rotten tubs afloat until we can get back."

"Get back to where?" Louis asked Alphonse.

"Listen," said Alphonse. "I've got a plan. If we can go up the coast to the Bay of Fundy, we can get to the St. John River. Some Acadians left before the Deportation and went across the Bay and up the St. John River. If we can get there, we can join them. Maybe we can even get the Indians to help us take back our Land from the British."

"Well, we have to get there first," Louis said hesitantly. He was concerned about the seaworthiness of these boats. He confessed to himself that he was afraid that they would not stay afloat long enough to get them there, especially with the winter storms that'll soon be upon them. He hated to take such a chance with all these lives, but there was no other choice. They would have to take the chance. Maybe they could make it before the storms hit.

"That's a good plan," said Jean. "Let's make it happen."

"Yes," said Fabien, rubbing his hands together. "The sooner we join other Acadians the better. We'll be able to find our families."

Maybe Fabien was right, Louis thought. If we can find out where they are and get a good ship, we can go get them. I would walk through fire to get to Emmeline. In his mind's eye he could see the moonlight sparkling in her hair as the pale silver of the harvest moon caressed her face. He could hear voice, soft and sweet as a summer breeze, "Remember, beyond the storm, the sun still shines." The words gave him hope. We'll get through this storm. We'll meet again beyond the storm where the sun still shines.

"Come on everybody!" Alphonse shouted. "Let's load up the boats. We're going home!"

The men met this with shouts of joy, but the shouts faded when they saw the condition of the boats.

"We can make it," Alphonse reassured the men.

"Fifty men go in the first boat!" Louis shouted. "Pick up supplies as you go on board. Alphonse will go with you. The rest will board the other boat with me."

The boats shoved off from the docks. Wind filled the sails as the little boats plowed through the waters of the bay into the open sea. They were overloaded, but the men were determined.

"Stay close to the coastline!" Louis shouted to Alphonse in the other boat. "Just in case."

"Don't worry about me!" Alphonse shouted back. "My boat's taking on water. But we'll be all right as long as we keep bailing!"

Louis went below to check on the water in his boat. There was water in the bottom.

"Start a bailing brigade!" Louis shouted at the men who were below. Half were on deck and half were below.

There was a moderate wind from the south and they made good headway. The men bailed water throughout the day and through the night. When morning came, the wind had turned, blowing strong and cold from the north.

The boats had to tack. Each time they turned with their side to the wind and waves, they took on water.

Over the crash of the waves against the hull, Louis heard Alphonse. "We can't go any farther! We'll have to beach! We're sinking!"

"We'll follow you!" Louis screamed above the wind and waves. "We're going to beach the boat!" Louis yelled to the men in the hole. "Get ready to abandon ship when you feel it hit bottom!"

Louis watched as Alphonse's boat approached the shore. It hit the outer sandbar, rolled on it's side, straightened, hit the second sand bar and started to break up with the pounding waves.

"Get ready!" Louis screamed as his boat approached the outer sandbar. His heart pounded in his throat.

The boat ground onto the sandbar with a sickening thud and rolled onto its side. The waves pounded the worm eaten hull mercilessly as it scraped and ground against the sandbar. Finally it was across and floating again, but it didn't have time to right itself before it hit the second sandbar. The boat slammed into it with a grinding, shudder. Louis held onto the mast as men were thrown into the water. Each wave crashed mercilessly against the rotten wood. Finally the boat broke apart with a shattering roar amid the cries of desperate men.

Cold water swirled around him. It tore at him, trying to pull the air from his lungs. He fought the grasping, pulling, tearing sea. Each time he gasped for air, waves would smash down on him and he would be surrounded with black water and white foam. Finally his feet touched bottom and he dragged himself to shore and collapsed on the sandy beach.

He was brought to his senses by Alphonse shouting, "Brother–in–law! You all right?"

Louis struggled to sit up. "Where's Jean and Fabien? Are they all right? Where are they?"

"Here they come," replied Alphonse. "They made it." Jean and Fabien staggered toward them. Jean fell to his knees and Alphonse ran to help him to his feet.

"Are you all right?" Louis asked.

"I'm all right," Jean answered as he coughed and choked. "I'm all right, now. What about the others?"

"Let's get everyone together and have a count." Louis struggled to get the words out. He sat in the sand and vomited salt water. As he waited for Alphonse to return, he wondered what to do next. They were shipwrecked, cold and without supplies and shelter. He closed his eyes and waited.

"Son of a bitch!" Louis heard Alphonse mutter. He opened his eyes and saw Alphonse walking slowly toward him. "I only count fifty–one. We lost half our men."

"Are you sure?" Louis asked, not believing what he had just heard. "Where are the bodies?"

"Don't know," Alphonse answered. "Guess they washed back out to sea. Current's running pretty strong."

The survivors wandered around in shock, looking for their relatives and friends. Louis sat in stunned silence. How could they have lost all those men? Dead.

Fabien came to Louis holding a young boy in his arms. "He was alive when I found him." He gently laid him down. "We can't just leave him here," he sobbed as he started digging in the sand with his hands.

Louis helped with the digging until his hands were raw. How could it come to this? They rolled the body into the shallow trench and pushed sand over it.

Fabien stood up, his fingers bleeding. He shivered as tears rolled down his cheeks.

Alphonse walked up to Louis. "We have to get these men off the beach and out of the wind," he said. "If we don't take care of them, we won't have enough to fight the British when we get back."

Louis was soaked and shivering. The cold wind cut through his wet clothing, soaking up his body's warmth. He felt as though the wind was hungry for human life. It had taken life from half of their group and given their bodies over to the hungry, crashing sea to devour. But that was not enough. It was trying to suck the life sustaining warmth from him and those around him. "Let's go inland and try to make a fire or find some friendly Indians," he said, his teeth chattering.

"Hey!" Louis heard a shout. "Look!"

Someone pointed around the curve of the beach. Louis stumbled toward the man who was shouting, while he tried to catch his breath, still choking. The beach made a sweeping curve. Beyond was a bay. He could see boats at anchor. What luck! Louis thought. In all this wilderness, to be stranded near a settlement! This is too good to be true!

"This looks like a path," Alphonse shouted.

The group shuffled and stumbled down the path, helping each other along. After awhile they saw houses.

As they approached the houses, they were met by men with muskets who shouted at them in English.

"Where's Joseph?" Louis asked.

"Here he comes," said Jean.

"Talk to these men," Louis said to Joseph, "and find out where we are."

Joseph walked up to the townspeople and talked to them. He returned to Louis. "We're in Virginia. This is the village of Hampton. They thought we were enemies coming to raid their village. I told them that we were shipwrecked. That we're not enemies and we have no weapons. They'll allow us to approach their village and they'll make a fire for us to warm up. But we must stay outside their village."

The fire felt good. It reminded Louis of home and the times he stood before the huge hearth. He wondered where his father had landed. He thought about his mother and sister. Where were they? His mother was not in good health. He hoped that she was taken care of. Surely the British would not be so cold hearted as to have treated the women and children badly. There were babies with the women.

His thoughts wondered back to Emmeline. Was she cold and hungry? If only I could be at her side to take care of her. He imagined holding her in his arms. He had to find her! He would devote his life to finding her.

Yes, he would make the British pay for what they had done. The Governor would be hung in the square where everybody would see, and his body left to rot. The British soldiers would feel the points of the Acadian's bayonets.

"I'm hungry," Fabien's voice brought Louis out of his thoughts—back to reality.

"Here comes the village people again with muskets," Alphonse said. "What do they want now? Why can't they bring us some food?"

"Where's Joseph?" Louis asked. "Joseph, come talk to these people before they decide to shoot us."

Joseph talked with the village people for quite a while with both sides motioning and waving their arms. Finally Joseph came back to the group of Acadians. "These people are Irish and hard to understand. They don't speak the same as the British soldiers. Now, they think we're pirates. I told them we were not pirates, that we are people like they are and we need help. They said, if we were not pirates, where were our women and children? I told them the British had separated the women and children from the men—that we didn't know where they were."

"What did they say to that?" Louis asked.

"They didn't believe me. They don't think the British would do something as cruel as that. They're suspicious," Joseph said. "I told them that if we were pirates, why didn't we have weapons?" Joseph continued. "I told them we needed food. They said they will go back to the village and think about it."

"What's wrong with these people?" Alphonse demanded as he hit his fist into the palm of his hand and clenched his teeth. "Can't they see who we are?"

"These people are far from civilization," Louis observed. "Naturally, they're suspicious. They have to defend their village. They have women and children to protect."

"Yes," said Jean as he rubbed his hands in front of the fire. "At least they have weapons to protect themselves. We had nothing."

The men of the village were gone a long time. Well, at least we're now dry and warm, Louis thought, but we need something to eat.

Finally after what seemed like an eternity, Louis saw the men returning, still carrying their weapons. "Joseph, go out and meet them." He was getting very agitated by this time. I'm glad Joseph knows English, he thought. They should respect a white haired man.

"I'll go with Joseph," Alphonse said impatiently. "I'll get them to make up their mind."

"No!" Louis said emphatically. "You stay here and let Joseph go alone. Don't cause trouble."

After more arm motions and loud talk, Joseph returned.

"Well, what did they say this time?" Alphonse asked.

Joseph shook his head slowly. "These people are hopeless. They're still suspicious of us. They now think we might be Libertines and they need to get rid of us. They said that if we do not cause trouble and agree to leave they have a plan for us. But first, they want to know how much money we have among us."

"Those bastards!" shouted Alphonse. "This is a shakedown."

Louis took a deep breath and slowly let the air out between his teeth. "What choice do we have?" he said slowly as he rubbed his eyes. "Alphonse, go among the men and collect whatever money they have. Explain that this is our only option."

Alphonse returned looking downtrodden.

"What's the matter?" Louis asked.

"The men don't want to give up their money."

"Joseph," Louis said with a sigh. "Try to find out what the plan is."

Joseph returned looking glum. "They won't tell us until they know how much money we have."

"What do you think, Alphonse?" Louis asked with a sigh. "If all they wanted was to take our money, they would just kill us and take it."

"I'll explain to the men that this is our only hope of getting out of here." Alphonse said, waving his arms in frustration. "I guess we have to tell these bastards how much money we have so we can hear their plan."

While the village men stood with their muskets pointed toward the group of Acadians, Alphonse circulated among the men with Fabien collecting the money in his coat. When they were finished, Fabien counted the money.

"How much do we have?" asked Louis.

"We have 400 pieces of eight," answered Fabien.

"Joseph, tell them that we have 400 pieces of eight," Louis said. "I don't know what that will buy us."

When Joseph returned from telling the village men what they had collected, he motioned for Louis and Alphonse to confer with him.

"They said that for 400 pieces of eight, they will sell us a ship and will supply it for us with good supplies," Joseph said. "But, I don't trust them. Suppose they take our money and they don't fulfill their end of the bargain?"

"Yes," said Louis. "You think if we tell them we'll give them 200 now and 200 when we board the ship, they'll agree?"

Joseph didn't stay long, this time and he came back with a solemn look. "They won't agree. They say they must have the money now or there's no deal."

"Those bastards!" Alphonse grunted. "Tell them we'll give them 200 now and show them the rest. But they don't get it 'till we get the ship."

Joseph came back and reported, "They said to give them all the money now or the deal's off and we'll have to leave…walk down the beach and never come back…or we'll be shot on sight. They said to hurry…they're tired of haggling."

"We're not in any position to bargain," said Louis. He didn't like the tone of what was going on but they left the Acadians no room to negotiate. They had to play along and hope that this was not a trick.

"What do you think?" Louis asked Jean and Alphonse.

"Well, I don't think we have any choice," said Jean.

"Yes," said Alphonse. "But, if they take our money and not give us the ship, that means they'll want to kill us."

"If they wanted to kill us they could kill us now and take our money," Louis said. "But then maybe they don't want our blood on their hands. They could take our money and send us down the beach to starve."

"That's right," Jean said. "Either way, we're dead."

"Let's think about this…" Alphonse rubbed his chin as if in deep thought. "We have twice as many men than they have. They only have one shot from their musket before they have to reload. They have no swords. If we have to, we can rush them. Some of us will be killed, but it's better than all of us dying."

Louis took a deep breath and let out a sigh. "Looks like that's our only option," he said sadly. "But maybe it won't come to that. I heard that the Irish were religious people. Joseph go back and tell the village men that we are giving them the money, but we are placing our fate in God's hands and that God will punish them if they betray us.

"But first, Alphonse, go to our men and tell them of our plan to rush the village men if we have to. Tell them that you will shout the word 'ATTACK' if we are to rush them."

After the men had enough time to digest the plan, Louis motioned to Joseph. "All right. Bring them the money."

Fabien went with Joseph, holding the money in his coat. When they approached the village men, one of them stepped forward and grabbed the coat with the money from Fabien. They then went back to the village while some stayed behind pointing their muskets at the Acadians. Fabien walked backward to the group of Acadians.

"Why did you do that?" Alphonse asked Fabien.

"I was afraid to turn my back on them." Fabien said, his voice shaking. "I don't trust them. Did you see how they grabbed my coat? They took my coat. How will I keep warm?"

"Be tough," Alphonse growled. "How are you going to fight the British if you're not tough."

"I don't want to fight." Fabien said softly under his breath.

"Don't worry," Louis said to Fabien. "We'll get your coat back."

"Joseph," Louis continued. "Go to the townspeople and ask to get Fabien's coat back."

"No need to," Joseph said.

Louis looked up and saw one of the townspeople throw the coat toward them.

"Please get it for me," Fabien asked no one in particular.

"I'll get it," said Alphonse. "I'm not scared of them." He walked toward the men holding the muskets. Striding confidently toward the coat, he walked passed it toward the village men. They raised their muskets and pointed them toward Alphonse. He stopped and glared at the men holding the guns. Louis watched, his heart pounding. Alphonse slowly turned and walked to the coat, picked it up, strode back, and handed it to Fabien.

"Thank you," Fabien said.

"That was a dumb thing to do," said Jean. "You could've gotten yourself killed."

Yes, thought Louis. But that was Alphonse. I'll have to try to keep him reined in before he gets us all killed. But that's not an easy thing to do.

Alphonse swaggered back and forth in front of the Acadians as they cheered him on.

The cheering stopped as a contingency of villagers approached. They were smiling, and although Louis was suspicious, there was also hope. Joseph went forward to meet them.

When Joseph came back to the Acadians, he too was smiling. This looks good, thought Louis, but we must remain cautious.

"Well, what did they say?" asked Louis.

"They have a ship that's large enough for us with plenty of room and they'll give us fresh supplies. We need a work party to load the supplies, but we'll still be under the watch of the musket holders. They still don't trust us, but don't want to cross us up because I think they're afraid of us."

"Good," said Louis. "Let's hope they stay that way." He looked at Alphonse. "Circulate among the men and tell them, and I mean you too, not to say or do anything to get them mad. We need to get out of here."

"Joseph, take Jean and get a work party together to load the supplies on board the ship," Louis barked.

After all of the supplies had been loaded on board, Louis stood looking at the ship that was at anchor in the bay. It looked good enough, but until he went aboard and inspected it, he couldn't tell. All of the men were on board except Jean, Joseph and him. The long-boat was on the beach waiting. Joseph shook hands with what appeared to be the mayor of the village. The man then walked up to Louis and shook hands with him. He said something but Louis didn't understand.

"All right, big brother," Jean called to Louis. "Let's go."

The bay was smooth as glass as they rowed to the ship. Would this ship be the one that would be their ticket to freedom and to finding their families? Louis made a promise to himself that he would do whatever it would take to find his beloved Emmeline and get their families back again. Even if it meant gathering an army and fighting the British.

Louis climbed up the rope ladder to the deck. "All right, haul up the longboat," he commanded. He looked around for Alphonse.

"Well, how does the ship look?" Louis asked anxiously.

"Not too bad," Alphonse answered. "We can get to the Bay of Fundy and the St. John River. Then we can join our brothers and raise an army. The Indians will be happy to help us fight the British. We can do it!"

"Well, first we have to get there," Louis said. "So let's get started.

A light breeze pushed them forward and they sailed out of the harbor and into the ocean. Night was falling, and after a full daily ration, combined with the events of the day, the men were exhausted. There was enough room below deck for all of the men to sleep.

After an inspection of the ship, Louis agreed with Alphonse. He had seen better but the hull appeared to be strong enough as long as they didn't encounter any gales.

"Fabien and I will take the first watch," Louis told Alphonse. "You and Jean can take the second. Each watch will need five or six able bodied men to tend the sails. I'll pick my men and you can pick yours."

"All right, brother–in–law. I'll take it down below and get some rest. Send someone to wake me when it's time."

The sea was a series of long, low swells. A slight breeze was blow-ing from the North. The ship was able to tack easily without having to fight the waves. I wish we could move faster, Louis thought, but at least this way the ship will hopefully hold together long enough to get to the river.

Louis' mind drifted as he watched the western sky fade from red to purple as darkness closed in around the little ship. He thought about the last time that he held Emmeline in his arms. Her hair fell in loose curls on her shoulders. The perfume of her very being had intoxicated him. He longed for her. Oh, how he longed to hold her. But instead they were unknown worlds apart. Unknown. That was the hardest part. Where was she? Where could I go to find her? It's strange how life is, he thought, how you should never take anything for granted. When he held her and kissed her that night, he took for granted that he would hold and kiss her the next night. Why, God, why? Why would you do this to me? Have I done something so bad that I deserve this, or is this some cruel joke?

"Louis." The word woke him from his reverie. He turned to see Fabien.

"Do you think we'll ever see our families again?" Fabien asked.

"Somehow, somewhere," Louis answered softly.

"I miss my family," Fabien said, wiping a tear from his eye.

"I know," said Louis.

"I was thinking about the pair of sheep I gave you," mused Fabien. "I raised them from little lambs. They would have had newborns in the spring. Emmeline would have been able to make warm things from the wool. I loved them, that's why I gave them to you. It hurts me to think of it, but the British probably killed and ate them."

"Why does God let this happen?" Louis grunted, trying not to let Fabien hear the choke in his voice. He gave the wheel of the boat a couple of turns to take a new tack.

"Bad things happen," Fabien answered softly, "because God gives everyone the freedom to choose between right and wrong. If God didn't give us this freedom, he wouldn't be any better than the British governor. We'd be like slaves. This is not a perfect world, Louis, but God didn't make it that way. We did."

"You're right," Louis said. "I never thought of it that way. Then it's up to us to make it right. It's up to us to raise an army, kill the bastards and take our land back."

"You don't get it, do you? Killing is not the answer," Fabien said sadly. He was silent and then added sharply. "How many lives is the price of our land?"

Louis shot back, "But it's our country! The British took it from us and scattered us to the wind! What about my family? What about your family? What about Emmeline? If the British die, they deserve to die!"

"Maybe we can negotiate with the British when we get back. Maybe we can work something out."

"Dream on, my friend," said Louis. "If the British see us, they'll want to put us in prison, or worse. They don't want to talk."

"Maybe you're right. It's probably too late," said Fabien sadly. "I guess we can never go back. Even if we take our land back it would never be the same."

Louis felt anger welling within him. "We will take our land back! We'll make them pay! When we clean our land of the British scum, our families will come back and everything will be the same as it was before."

"I'm sorry, Louis," Fabien choked on the words. "That part of our lives is behind us. Our houses are burned. Our animals are taken and killed. Our families are scattered. We may never see them again. I was fooling myself into thinking…"

"Sometimes I wonder about you, Fabien," Louis answered almost under his breath. "If you think that way, why are you coming back with us?"

Fabien put his hand on Louis' shoulder. "Because you're my friend. Besides, where could I go?" He was quiet for a while, looking into the star studded sky, then he continued. "Louis, would you do something for me?"

"Sure," answered Louis. "What is it?"

"I'm embarrassed to ask you this, but could you put your arms around me? I feel so alone."

Louis looked around to see if any of the men on deck were looking. Then he put his arms around Fabien and held him. Fabien put his head on Louis' shoulder. Louis could feel the sobs. The water sparkled in the moonlight as if someone had sprinkled it with silver. A highway of silver stretching to the horizon—to the destiny of all the men on the little ship.

Louis patted Fabien softly on the back. "Someone I love very dearly once told me that beyond the storm, the sun still shines. We'll brave the storm, my friend. We'll come out beyond the storm"

Louis awoke to the crashing of waves on the side of the little ship. He got up, steadied himself and climbed the ladder to the deck. Alphonse was at the wheel.

"What's going on?" Louis shouted over the gale. He slipped across the rain soaked deck. The sky was a leaden gray and rain stung his face by the force of the wind.

"This is going to be a bad one, brother–in–law," Alphonse shouted back. "Smell the wind. There's going to be ice in it before it's over. I hope this old tub holds together. We've trimmed the sails to just the jib."

The seas grew with billows building upon each other. Every time a wave crashed over the deck, the ship shuddered. Louis stood next to Alphonse helping him hold the wheel. "Think we can make it?" Louis shouted in his ear.

"Don't know," Alphonse shouted back.

Just then a monstrous wave crashed across the deck. Louis held on to the wheel as his feet were swept from under him. "You all right, Alphonse?"

"Better get below, brother–in–law," Alphonse shouted.

Louis looked around just as another monster wave crashed across the deck. He heard the splintering of wood as part of the superstructure was torn away.

"Damn!" shouted Alphonse. "My two men just got washed overboard! Poor bastards. Nothing we can do. Hope they make it to shore."

Someone shouted from the hole. "We're taking on water!"

"We'll have to beach her!" Alphonse shouted. "Hope we do a better job this time."

Louis squinted to see as rain stung his face. Just then the torrent stopped for a few seconds and he thought he saw an opening in the shoreline. Was that a pass to a bay? "Wait a minute!" he shouted to Alphonse. "Think I saw a pass!"

"Yes, looks like it could be," Alphonse cupped his hands to his mouth, then quickly grabbed the wheel again. "What have we got to lose," he screamed above the gale as he fought to turn the wheel.

Louis helped Alphonse struggling with the wheel. The ship nosed toward the breach in the coastline. I hope there's no reef or sandbar across the pass, if it actually is a bay, Louis thought. The ship edged closer and closer to the opening. We'll either crash into a reef or sandbar and break up, or sail into protected waters. As the ship entered the opening Louis held his breath. This was either life or death for all of us, he thought.

The little ship crossed smoothly through the opening into protected waters.

"We'll beach her on the shore and repair her after the storm," Alphonse said.

As the rolling of the ship and the crashing of the waves subsided, Jean came on deck to see what was happening. "Fabien is leading everyone in prayer. It seems to have worked. Where are we?" he asked.

"We're in a protected bay. Go below and tell the men not to worry," Louis said. "Tell 'em we're gonna beach the ship and repair it after the storm. Tell 'em to prepare for a beaching but it won't be hard."

Alphonse turned the ship so that the jib filled with wind and headed the bow directly toward the beach. Louis grabbed the wheel with both hands to brace himself. "Hold on!" Alphonse shouted as he also braced himself. The ship growled as the keel touched the bottom, smoothly ground to a stop then rolled partly on its side.

"Well, brother–in–law, we did it!" Alphonse grinned as he slapped Louis on the back. "That wasn't bad at all. When the storm's over we need to right the ship with timbers, repair the superstructure, find some pine to make pitch and start repairing this baby. There's a lot of work to do if we're going to make this tub seaworthy. Hope we find tools on board to be able to cut trees and shape timbers."

"Alphonse," Louis said. His legs were still shaky. "We can't risk any more storms in this ship. We'll have to wait until after the winter storms are over before we set sail again."

"No," Alphonse said. "We can't wait."

"Think about it," Louis answered. "We can't risk any more storms, even if we repair it. When this gale's over, we need to go ashore and make shelters for the winter."

"If we go on, we won't need to make shelters," argued Alphonse.

"It will take us a while to repair the ship. We might get caught without shelter," said Louis.

"We'll waste a whole winter," countered Alphonse. "When we could be getting an army together."

"We can't take any more chances with these men," said Louis. "We have to help them survive, and we have a better chance on land than on the ocean."

Alphonse grunted. "Well, it'll be tough just trying to keep alive here when winter sets in, but oh, all right. Guess we have a better chance on land than at sea with this old tub. Besides, we can make fires to keep warm here."

"Then you agree?" Louis wiped the salt spray from his eyes.

"I'd rather keep going!" Alphonse slammed his fist into his hand. "But all right. We can repair the ship in the spring. In the meantime we need to try to get food to survive."

If we survive until spring, Louis thought…if we survive until spring.

CHAPTER 7

*J*oseph, in his negotiations for the ship, had included tools for its repairs. But for the time being it was more important to build shelters for the winter. The men built crude lean–tos just before the snow started to fly. Any repairs to the ship would have to wait until the spring. The priority now was to survive.

There was plenty of firewood. They had moved off of the beach and were in the forest where the trees afforded some protection. The men obtained fresh water by melting the snow, but the supplies that had been loaded on the ship were now exhausted. Some of the men made snares and were able to trap a few animals, which they shared with everyone, but that wasn't enough. Slowly, the men became weaker and were not able to venture into the forest to try to snare game.

Fabien and a few of the men walked along the beach and brought back seaweed. "There is nourishment in seaweed. We need to eat it," Fabien declared. Everyone tried to eat. Some held it down but others vomited it up, which made them weaker.

Louis sat under the shelter of their lean–to and shivered, even though a fire was burning. His gut ached from hunger. Is this how it's all going to end, he thought? Fabien lay next to him on the bare ground.

"I'm hungry," Fabien said. "The raw seaweed didn't help. I wonder if boiling the seaweed would work better?"

"No," Louis mumbled. "Might make things worse."

"Some of the men are chewing their leather belts," Fabien continued.

"Sounds like a good idea right now," replied Louis. "We've got to get something to eat or we'll all starve."

Alphonse stumbled to where they were and dropped on the ground by the fire. "Doesn't look good," he mumbled. "Just made a walk through the camp. Lots of sick people. Five dead. There'll be more if we don't get food."

"What can we do?" Louis strained to get the words out. "Can't just sit here and die.

Jean followed Alphonse. "Ground's too hard to bury the dead. We pulled them out into the forest, away from the camp. Covered them with branches. Can't help it, but the wild animals probably will eat them."

The thought crossed Louis' mind, why let the animals eat them? Would it be wrong if we ate them instead? Meat is meat. Why waste it?

What am I doing? I can't believe I'm thinking this. Louis shook his head.

"You know what I'm thinking?" Alphonse said suddenly.

"Don't say it," Louis said. "We can't do that."

"What are you talking about?" Alphonse replied. "Why don't you want me to say it? You feeling all right?"

"Sorry," replied Louis, feeling ashamed. "What are you thinking?"

"We can put out some fishing lines and catch fish," Alphonse said. "We can make hooks with sea shells and tie pieces of cloth on them for bait."

"Wait!" said Louis excitedly. "The jib sail. We can punch holes in it so the water can sift through and use it for a seine."

"What will we do in the spring?" asked Jean. "When we want to sail?"

"We can make do without a jib if we have to," Louis said raising as much enthusiasm as he could. "If we don't, there may not be a spring for us."

"Good idea!" Alphonse said as he stood up. "Let's do it."

The four men, Louis, Jean, Alphonse and Fabien, struggled to the ship and removed the jib from the locker where it was stored. Taking turns, they punched holes in it with a spike until they were exhausted.

At the water's edge, they took their positions, two at each end, and started to drag the makeshift seine out into the water. Each step was agonizing as their weakened bodies fought against the cold waves and the force of the water against the canvas. Louis groaned as he fought with what little strength was left. Every muscle in his body ached. Sharp pains shot through his gut. Finally they pulled the seine to the shore and collapsed on the sand.

"We've got to get up," Louis heard Alphonse say.

Struggling to their feet they were amazed at the fish that they had caught. The four dragged the canvas and the fish back to the camp. Exhausted, they fell on the ground and called to the others to come and eat.

Some ate them raw. Others held them over the fire on sticks. Everyone had something to eat. Fabien brought a pot from the ship and made soup with some of the fish using melted snow. Jean helped him feed this to the ones who were too sick to eat the fish.

After resting and feeling their strength returning, the four went back to the beach and pulled in another catch of fish.

Later, in their lean–to, Louis, Alphonse, Jean and Fabien, knelt and thanked God for their good fortune.

"I'm still not full," said Alphonse, "but by tomorrow I'll feel strong. We can get more fish. Yes, we're going to make it through the winter."

During the night, howling wind and frigid blasts awakened Louis. The air was filled with white. He sat up shivering. The wind had blown the fire out and the snow had put out the embers. Stinging snow blew and swirled into the lean–to.

Louis reached over and shook Alphonse. "Wake up." Louis' voice betrayed his fears. "Wake up, Alphonse."

"What…?" Alphonse shivered a reply. He sat up, rubbing his eyes and shaking. "Damn! What next? I'm about to freeze."

By this time Jean and Fabien were awake.

"We'll never get the fire started in this blizzard," shivered Jean.

"We're all going to die," moaned Fabien.

"No, we're going to make it," Alphonse said.

"We need to huddle together to share our body heat and use our coats to cover ourselves," Louis said between shivers. His fingers and toes were numb.

Alphonse rubbed his hands together trying to generate heat by friction.

The four huddled together, covered with their coats. A blanket of white built up over them as it blew into the lean–to. The snow muffled the sound, but they could still hear the howl of the wind. At first they shivered and moaned, then the shivering came in painful spurts as they tried to share each others body heat. They fitfully napped. Each time Louis awoke, he listened to hear if the others were breathing. No one spoke so as to conserve energy. There was nothing to gain by speaking. Their whole psyche was devoted to personal survival.

Louis lost track of time. The hours slipped by in slow agony. At first he dreaded what he thought was inevitable death, then he actually welcomed it. His mind started playing tricks on him. He thought that he saw Emmeline standing near him, brown curls flowing softly over her shoulders. She smiled and held out her hand toward him. "Don't give up," he seemed to hear her say. "I love you. Come and find me. I'm waiting for you." She slowly faded away until there was only darkness and the howl of the wind. I won't give up, he thought. I'll find you, my love. We won't have the little home I built for you, but we'll have each other. That's what matters. No matter where we'll be, we'll still have our love. I'll live. I'll find you…I'll find you.

The cold slowly seeped into Louis' bones. But now something was different. It was the sound of silence. Louis peeked out from under the coats and saw only white. Snow covered them.

"What's going on?" Alphonse asked as he tried to see out from under the coats.

"Are we dead yet?" Fabien moaned.

"Get back under here," Jean said weakly. "We'll freeze."

"No, wait." Louis forced the words, his teeth chattering. "Storm's over. Wind's stopped. Try to start the fire."

Louis pushed the snow away and stood up on shaky legs. He fell to his knees then struggled up again, clutching his coat around himself. It was morning. The sunlight sparkled on a world of white. They had survived the night.

The cold felt like a sharp knife. His feet were numb. He staggered through knee–deep snow and cleared it from the charred wood where the fire had once been. Slowly and painfully he somehow got the fire started. They dug around in the snow, found the firewood they had stashed, and stoked the fire. Soon flames were leaping and warmth was seeping into Louis' flesh. He could finally feel his fingers. They hurt. Afraid that he might see his toes blackened with frostbite, he took off his boots. His toes were all right, but the pain in his feet was unbearable as they thawed in the warmth of the fire. Soon Louis saw other fires in the camp as smoke curled skyward.

After they felt sufficiently thawed out, Louis, Alphonse, Jean and Fabien, struggled through the deep snow to the other lean–tos to check on the other men and help them build fires.

Many of the men and boys had either frozen or died from sickness during the night. They helped drag the dead into the woods and cover them with snow.

Alphonse commented that there were only twenty–three men left. He lamented that there wouldn't be enough to fight the British. "We need to get to the St. John River and meet the others before we all die," he said as he wrung his hands.

"We need to get out of here alive," Louis said as he soaked up the fire's warmth.

"Wait," Alphonse said cautiously in a low voice.

Louis turned to see what it was that Alphonse saw. A small group of Indians approached the clearing from the woods.

Knowing sign language from trading with the Micmacs in Acadia, Louis raised his hand in peace. The Indians returned the sign. The Natives approached Louis and after seeing the sad state of affairs, invited the Acadians to their village to share in their food. Louis readily accepted the invitation.

The scraggly group of Acadians staggered after the Indians. After stopping several times to rest along the way, they came upon a native village. Curious women and children met them and stared. The Acadians followed their hosts to a large log building.

On the earthen floor, in the middle of the building, was a fire. Directly above it was a hole in the roof through which the smoke rose. The only light came from the open doorway, the hole in the roof and the fire.

Because Louis was able to communicate with sign language, he was led to the chief, who sat by the fire. Louis asked for permission to sit, which was granted.

The chief asked who they were and why they were there.

Louis answered that their land was taken from them by British warriors, the same ones who were wanting to take the Indian's land. He also told the old chief that they had to repair their ship so they could return and join other warriors to take back their land. They had to wait until spring to repair their ship, but they had no food.

The chief stared at Louis as if trying to gauge if he were telling the truth. The old man then asked Louis if he was the chief warrior and where were their weapons.

Louis told him that yes, he was the chief warrior. He said that the British had tricked them, had taken their weapons and had banished them from their lands.

The old chief then talked to the men in the council. After a lively discussion with his council, the chief told Louis that the Acadians were brave warriors. He would let them stay in the village with them and would feed them, but when the weather warmed in the spring, they must leave.

The chief again talked to the council. Then he turned and looked intently at Louis. Again, he told Louis that they were brave warriors. He then said that he would like to smoke the pipe with him.

A ceremonial pipe was filled with tobacco and the chief lit it with a burning stick. He then puffed on the pipe and handed it to Louis who took a puff and choked on the smoke. Louis handed the pipe back. The old chief smiled.

CHAPTER 8

Spring came to the Indian village. The sun was brighter and the warm breezes from the south pushed the snow northward. The Natives, true to their promise, had supplied the Acadians with food and shelter through the winter. There was only one death among the Acadians after they moved in with the Indians, a severely frost bitten boy. Louis noted sadly that there were only twenty–two survivors out of the original one hundred and fifty.

The men busied themselves repairing the ship. The old chief gave his blessing by allotting some of his braves to work with the Acadians.

On the spring tide, the Indians all showed up to help the Acadians push the ship into deep water. Supplies of food and water, gifts from the tribe, were loaded on board. The ship sat at anchor in the bay.

The chief declared that they would have a dance to celebrate the repair of the ship and a farewell to the Acadians. Two of the men decided to stay with the Indians. They each had fallen in love with native women. They would have to go through a ritual and a test before being accepted into the tribe, but that would have to wait until after the rest of the Acadians departed.

The night of the celebration, the native women cooked up a feast of corn mush and venison. The braves did a celebration dance around the fire to the beat of drums and hand clapping. After the dance, the pipe was passed between Louis and the chief.

The next morning, the Acadians bade farewell to their hosts and their two countrymen. Alphonse and Jean had gone ahead to prepare the ship for sailing. Louis and Fabien were the last to board the longboats.

Louis thanked the chief for saving their lives. He told the old chief that he had nothing to give him but his thanks and good will. Fabien stepped forward, slipped a leather strap with a gold crucifix over his head and handed it to the old man.

"Tell the chief that this is powerful medicine of the Great Spirit," Fabien said to Louis. "Tell him that my father gave it to me."

Louis told the old Indian what Fabien had said. The old man smiled at Fabien. He pressed it against his chest then slipped it over his head.

As they got on the longboat that was to take them to the ship, Louis turned toward the white haired chief. He raised his hand in peace then shoved off.

From the ship, Louis looked toward the beach at the group of Indians standing on the shore. He felt compassion for them, knowing that one day settlers would take their land and force them to leave as the British had done to his people. He knew that the Indians would not leave peacefully. Many brave warriors would die.

As the sails filled with wind and the ship bit through the water, Louis held up his hand in peace. He didn't know if the old chief could see it, but he thought he saw a hand on the shore also raised.

Why can't men live in harmony with their fellow man, he thought? He wondered how long the tribe would be able to live their lives in peace. Bowing his head, he said a prayer for the people who had reached out to them when they were in need. Louis also said a prayer of thanksgiving to God that there still were people like this tribe who wanted to invest in life rather than death—who would share their meager wealth rather than destroy for greed.

The little ship pressed northward through calm, sunny seas. The spirits of the men rose with each passing day.

"Hey, brother–in–law," Alphonse said cheerily. "You can almost feel and smell our homeland. When we meet our brothers on the St. John River, we'll get an army together and take back our lands."

"Yes," Louis agreed, although his heart wasn't in it. The long winter had given him time to think about things. He didn't feel the hate he had felt before. He only felt sorrow when he thought about the price the Acadians had already paid. How many more lives would it take to get our country back? It could never be the same. We could never go back in time. But then, defeating the British in Acadia might be the only way to find out where they had sent Emmeline and their families.

Louis looked out over the sea glistening in the sunlight. He raised his hands and let them drop despairingly at his side. "I wonder where they sent our families," he said.

"Don't worry, brother–in–law," Alphonse replied. "We'll find them. We'll make Governor Lawrence send ships to get them back…then we'll execute him to pay for what he's done."

"No," Fabien said as he walked up behind them. "Killing him won't undo the wrong he did. We must show them what compassion is."

"The British don't know what compassion is and they'll never learn," replied Alphonse.

"We're all human," said Fabien. "The British were only doing what their king told them to do."

"I don't know if the King of England even knows," Alphonse replied, his hands at his side, clenching and unclenching his fists. "I think Lawrence wanted us out so he would be more powerful."

"It doesn't really matter now, does it?" Louis said quietly. "What really matters is, what can we do to get our families back? If there would be any way other than killing…but if that's the only way…

The little ship entered the Bay of Fundy and a close watch began along the coastline looking for the river. They followed close to the western coastline fearing that they might be seen by British warships from Annapolis–Royal across the bay.

Just when they had thought that they must have missed the river and were getting ready to turn back, the lookout shouted. They trimmed the sails as Louis turned the little ship toward where the river entered the bay.

"We're in luck," Jean shouted. "The tide is rising and flowing into the river."

The bow of the vessel cut through the water, as they pushed up the river. Everyone watched the riverbanks in anticipation of seeing the fort. As they rounded a bend in the river, a log structure appeared on the starboard side, surrounded by a log parapet. A cheer went up from the men lining the railing.

The ship dropped anchor near the bank and the two longboats lowered over the side. Louis, Alphonse and Jean, on the first boat to land, jumped on the bank and ran toward the fort. The gate was opened and the courtyard was empty.

"Hello," shouted Alphonse. They waited. There was no reply.

Louis wandered around the compound. It was empty—no one. The storeroom had a supply of food and the armory was filled with arms and ammunition. Louis noted that there were no cannons in the fort and no accommodations were made for them.

Alphonse and Jean handed out muskets and ammunition to the men. Alphonse tucked a pistol in his belt. Fabien wouldn't take any arms.

"Here, if you don't want a musket, at least take a pistol," Alphonse said forcefully as he pushed a pistol against Fabien's chest. "It's for your protection."

Fabien backed away. "No. It's for killing," he replied.

"That's the whole idea," Alphonse said. "The idea is to kill them before they kill you. But if you want to die, it's up to you." Alphonse stuck the pistol in his belt. He now had two pistols in his belt and he strutted around saying, "Let the British come now."

"What do you think, big brother?" Jean asked as he stood next to Louis and tucked a pistol into his belt, but not before making sure that it was loaded.

"I don't know," Louis replied, looking around nervously. He didn't have a good feeling about the whole scene. It was as if everyone in the fort had suddenly disappeared.

Alphonse strutted up and announced that he had made sure that the gate was closed and barred. The men milled around in the courtyard, fidgeting with their weapons.

"Look! Coming out of the forest!" someone shouted.

Louis climbed up to the walkway on the parapet. About a dozen men with shovels over their shoulders waived a white flag.

"Open the gate," ordered Alphonse.

The men approaching with the white flag stopped. Upon hearing French being spoken, one shouted, "Are you French?"

"We're Acadians," was the answer.

They flung down their shovels and ran toward the men in the stockade. "Brothers!" the cry went up with much hugging.

"What happened here?" Louis asked.

"Smallpox," was the answer. Then with a sigh of relief, a gaunt man with haunting eyes continued, "We thought you were British."

"I'll tell you what happened," another one of the men said wearily. "I'm Father Pierre."

They all went inside to the great room and the priest began his story: "We were over two hundred souls here last fall—trying to establish a force to resist the British until the French could join us from the west. We're all Acadians who escaped before the Exile. The men's families were left behind in Acadia. They thought they could return, chase the British out and be with their families again. Now they don't know where they are."

"We don't know where our families…" Louis started to speak but was interrupted by the priest.

"We successfully fought off a small British landing party before the winter set in," the priest continued, "Now, we're afraid a large British force will come to destroy us." The priest looked around and continued. "Which wouldn't be hard now.

"You see, during the winter, smallpox spread through the fort, killing all but what you see now. British couldn't have done a better job. We couldn't bury our dead until the ground thawed. We were burying the last of our dead when you came.

"I thought the British had returned to finish us off." The priest took a deep breath and let out a sigh. "But they will return."

Louis tried to say something but was interrupted again by the priest. "Then you aren't the reinforcements from the French, are you?"

When Louis finally had a chance to talk, he replied. "No, we're not French reinforcements. I think the French forgot about us. Our families were separated and scattered…don't know where."

"We'll help you fight off the British if they attack," Alphonse said as he patted one of his pistols.

"We're Acadians, just like you," Louis continued. "We were shipped to Carolina and we've been trying to get here ever since. We hoped we could join forces with you and other Acadians to take back our Country, but…"

"Where are the rest of your group?" the Priest interrupted. "Wasn't there more with you?"

"We started out with about a hundred and fifty and this is what we have left. Looks like we don't have enough for an army here," Louis said as he let his breath out in a whistle and looked around the room. "But you do have enough arms and ammunition here to hold off the British if they try to take us."

"They'll come," Father Pierre injected as he fingered a crucifix hanging on a gold chain around his neck. "They will. Our only hope is that the French troops will join us in time. But I don't think we can depend on them. They don't care about us Acadians or they wouldn't have let the British destroy us. I don't know if they even consider us French anymore."

"Well," Alphonse said as he joined in the conversation. "If they don't consider us their countrymen we don't need them or want them. We can join up with the Micmacs. They'll help us."

"They'll need arms and ammunition," Father Pierre broke in. "You saw what we have. Not enough for an army."

"I have a plan," Alphonse said as he hit the palm of his hand with his fist. "Listen. We can go up the river in the ship, as far as we can go, then head west on foot. Meet up with the French…"

"I thought you said you didn't want help from the French. Besides, that won't work," interrupted Louis.

"Why?" Alphonse shot back.

"Think," Louis replied. "We can't take all the ammunition with us when we leave the ship. Do you want to leave it for the British or unfriendly Indians to find? And we don't want to leave it here. I think you're just grasping at straws. We need a real plan. One that will work."

"Well, brother–in–law," Alphonse said sarcastically. "We don't want to just sit here, do we?"

Father Pierre broke in. "Fort Beauséjour on the north end of the Bay of Fundy is still in French hands. If we can sail without being intercepted by the British, we can join the French forces there."

"Well, that sounds like a real plan. One that will work. Do you think this plan will work, Louis?" Alphonse said, stressing each word. "If I had thought of it, would you think that I would be grasping at straws?"

"I'm sorry, Alphonse," Louis said. "I didn't mean it the way it sounded. I guess we're all kind of grasping at straws, right now."

"Apology accepted, brother–in–law," Alphonse said with a smile as he patted Louis on the back.

Father Pierre looked at Alphonse and smiled. "I have a small barrel of brandy that was given to me as a gift when I left Acadia. I've been saving it for the right occasion. Tonight we'll celebrate before we leave for the fort. We also have a store of smoked venison. We can't take it all with us so…"

"That's another plan that will work." Alphonse exclaimed as he jumped up. "Let's load up the ship tomorrow and start for the fort. But tonight there's drinks and a lot of good food."

Alphonse and Father Pierre walked off together. "Come on, Louis," Alphonse said looking back over his shoulder. "Let's start the celebration."

"Go ahead," Louis responded. "I'll join you later."

Louis climbed up to the parapet and looked out toward the ship that had brought them there. Everything seemed so peaceful now. How long will it last? What will it be like when they reach the fort? Will they be able to get the help they need to get their land back? To get their families back? To get Emmeline back?

Someone started singing and the celebration began. The aroma of food cooking soon filled the air. Louis was glad to see the men finally enjoying themselves. They deserve it he thought. The young boys that they had started with were no longer boys. The ordeals that they survived had made men out of them. How much of their childhood had been lost, never to be regained? He wondered how long it would be before they would be able to make merry again. Tomorrow they set sail for the fort.

Jean joined Louis on the parapet. He put his arm around his brother's waist. Together they gazed out at the thick green forest that surrounded them on three sides. Bird songs floated on the spring air.

"Tell me, big brother. Do you think we can do it?" Jean asked softly.

"Do what?"

"Can we somehow chase the British out of Acadia with the help of French forces?"

"I don't know. Don't even know if the French will want to help us. But we'll soon find out," Louis answered.

"Come join us," Jean said. "Let's celebrate. We've come this far."

"I'll join you in a minute." Louis' head was still swirling with unanswered questions. Could they somehow chase the British out of Acadia with the help of the French? How many Acadians were still alive? Where were their families? But the most pressing question was where was his beloved Emmeline? Was she still alive? She had to be! He knew that some day they would be with each other again.

The festivities went on into the night. As the brandy was consumed and the food eaten, the singing stopped and silence slowly settled over the little fort, save for the snoring of exhausted men.

The morning quietness was broken by the sound of cannon fire. Louis jumped up from his pallet, ran across the courtyard and climbed the parapet. Through the morning fog, he saw a glow. No! It couldn't be! Their ship was burning! Then through the crisp morning air he heard the boom of a cannon and a cannonball came crashing into the fort.

"The British! The British!" Came the yell. "The British are attacking."

Alphonse came running to meet Louis. "What's happening?"

"British warship!" shouted Louis. "Must have seen our ship."

By this time Jean arrived, his eyes wide with fright. "Cannon?" he gasped. "What can we do? We can't return the fire! We don't have any cannons."

"Find a safe place!" Alphonse yelled.

The cannon balls gave no safe haven. Each time a ball crashed into the fort Louis heard screams and groans. He crouched together with Alphonse and Jean. Strangely, Louis felt no fear. His only thought was survival.

Fabien came crawling toward them. "They're going to kill us!"

A cannon ball crashed through the parapet not five feet from where they were crouching. Louis sucked in his breath. What could they do? They couldn't even fight back. Would they just wait here to be killed?

Finally the volley stopped and there was an unearthly silence with only the groaning of the wounded and dying. Louis stood up to look around and saw a body cut in half by a cannon ball. He bent over and vomited.

"Are you all right?" Alphonse gasped as he too saw the body.

"Yes I'm all right." Louis gasped.

Joseph joined them. He was clearly shaken. His face was pale and his hands were shaking. "They've stopped."

"Come on," Louis said. "Let's get out of here and escape into the woods while we can."

As they started toward the rear of the fort facing the woods, they heard a staccato of musket fire.

"A landing party!" someone yelled.

Louis climbed back to the walkway on the parapet with Joseph and Jean. Alphonse and Fabien soon joined them. They saw flashes of gunfire in the fog. Soon shapes appeared as ghostly apparitions moving toward them in the mist. The British were between them and the river.

"Let's go!" yelled Fabien. "We don't have to kill. We can escape to the woods."

"Don't be a coward," Alphonse shot back. "We finally have a chance to fight those bastards! We can beat them!"

The crackle of musket fire erupted behind them. The British had surrounded them and cut them off from the forest! There was no escaping now. They had to face the British and hope that they could hold them off.

Louis aimed his musket at what appeared to be a shape in the fog and fired. He reloaded to fire again. Someone handed Fabien a musket, which he fired, then threw it down.

"What are you doing?" Alphonse shouted at Fabien.

"Why do we have to kill each other?" Fabien screamed.

"If we don't kill them, they'll kill us!" Alphonse yelled.

Fabien stood up and waved his arms above his head. "Stop the killing!" he shouted.

Louis dove at him, knocking him down. "What are you doing? You'll get yourself killed!"

"We've got to stop the killing!"

"Keep him down!" Alphonse yelled as he cupped his hands around his mouth.

"What do we gain by killing each other?" Fabian screamed above the noise of the gunfire.

"Stay down!" Louis shouted. He fired and was reloading when he heard Fabien gasp and fall.

"Fabien!" Louis shouted, falling to his knees by his friend. "Are you hit?"

"Yes," Fabien moaned, blood running from the side of his mouth.

Louis sat and gently placed Fabien's head in his lap. "You'll be all right."

"I'm scared," Fabien groaned.

"You'll be all right," Louis repeated. He opened Fabien's shirt. Blood oozed from a hole in his chest. With every breath, the blood bubbled. In horror Louis tore a piece of his shirt. His hand shook so badly he could barely stuff it in the gory hole.

"I'm going to die," Fabien gasped. "Tell my mamma and papa I love them." A smile slowly crossed his face. "It's beautiful," he whispered in Lewis' ear. "I'm not afraid anymore." He took a deep breath and gurgled. The grip on Louis' hand tightened then fell slack.

"No! Fabien! Don't die!" He cradled Fabien's head in his hands.

Louis had seen so much death before, but this was Fabien, a close friend he had grown up with. This can't be happening, he thought. It was so surreal—the noise—the cries of the dying—the smoke swirling around him—and now the cold grip of mortal fear. A silent scream welled up within him.

Louis felt an arm around his shoulders. He heard Alphonse say, "Now, let's kill these damn bastards."

"They're going to kill us all unless we surrender!" Louis yelled above the noise. "Look around at all the bodies! If we surrender we might be able to see our families again!"

"If we surrender we'll rot in prison!" Alphonse yelled back.

"If we're dead, we're dead forever! We might have a chance in prison!" Louis screamed.

"We'll never surrender!" shouted Alphonse. "They'll have to come get us!"

"Do you want me to marry your sister?"

"Yes!"

"Then get Jean, Joseph and Father Pierre," said Louis. He waited for what seemed like an eternity. The smell of gunpowder mixed with the sickeningly sweet aroma of blood seemed overpowering.

Finally Alphonse crawled back to Louis with Jean. "Father Pierre and Joseph are dead"

"We're going to surrender before we all die", Louis told Jean. "Do you agree?"

Jean nodded his head.

"You know, I'm doing this for you!" Alphonse shouted to Louis above the gunfire.

"Wait!" Someone shouted. "Father Pierre is dead, but I'm not! This is our fort and we'll fight to the last man!"

"Look around you! Do you want to stay here to die and lose?"

"We'll take as many enemy as we can!"

"You'll still lose! If we surrender we can live to one day conquer!"

"I'll ask my men what they want to do."

"Hurry! Men are dying!" Louis watched the man crawl away.

Alphonse pulled himself on his elbows to where he could speak in Louis' ear. "What's wrong with that bastard?"

"Thought you wanted to keep fighting?"

"Changed my mind. Want you to marry my sister."

Louis waited. Why is he taking so long? Louis thought. Men are dying! Hurry! A cannonball came crashing a few feet from where they crouched.

"They've started firing the cannon again!" Alphonse shouted.

"We have to do something fast!" Louis yelled back. "Or we'll all be dead!" He took Fabien's shirt and tied it to his musket. Fabien will finally have his way, he thought. There'll be no more killing.

"Call a cease-fire!" Louis screamed to Alphonse as another cannonball crashed nearby.

Alphonse bellowed above the gunfire, "Cease fire!" The shout was repeated along the parapet.

The fire from the fort stopped and Louis raised the flag of surrender. The fire from the British lines fell silent.

"Throw down your arms and leave the fort with your hands raised," a British officer shouted in French.

The men lay down their arms and slowly walked out of the fort.

"Who is in charge?" the British officer asked.

Everyone pointed to Louis.

"Wait!" Louis shouted. "Why me?"

The officer ordered Louis to approach him.

Louis hesitated, then slowly approached. His heart pounded in his throat. Fear squeezed his chest. The British! What would they do now? Why did everyone point to him as their leader? If the British thought that he was their leader, would they torture him? Would they kill him?

"You are not soldiers. Who are you?" the officer asked.

"Acadians," Louis answered, his voice shaking. "Neutrals who've been exiled from our country. We're not at war with England. We were only defending ourselves."

"You Acadians are not neutral. You refused to become British citizens. You are therefore our enemy. I am taking you as prisoners of war and you will be imprisoned in Halifax," the officer announced.

"Imprisoned?" Louis gasped. He knew that this would happen if they were captured, but it wasn't a reality until now. The full impact of what it meant now hit him with a force that shattered his will.

The Acadians were put below in the hole of the ship and the hatch closed and fastened. They were in total darkness.

"Where's my brother? Got to take care of my brother," Louis moaned.

"I'm here," Jean answered.

"Well, brother–in–law," Alphonse spoke from the darkness. "What now?"

Louis didn't answer. He had counted only sixteen who left the fort. He wondered what had happened to the wounded. Had they been left to die? Now there were only sixteen…out of one hundred and fifty in their original group plus two hundred from the fort before the sickness. Three hundred and fifty strong men had come out of Acadia and now only sixteen broken souls were returning. Returning to a cold prison cell. There was no hope of ever getting their country back. In the utter darkness of their surroundings, Louis surrendered to the inevitable. He broke out in a cold sweat. His strength melted from his body. Muscle seemed to turn to liquid and his legs folded under him. He collapsed on the floor with a groan.

"What's the matter, brother–in–law?" Alphonse asked as he knelt next to Louis.

"It's no use," Louis mumbled. "You were right. We should have let them kill us. Our lives are over. Everything's gone. We'll die in prison."

"No," Alphonse said. "I was wrong. I don't know how…but we'll find a way."

"They've destroyed us. Face it," Louis moaned as he held his head in his hands and gritted his teeth. He let out a moan of despair that was picked up by the other men—a moan that swirled in the clammy darkness—a darkness that seemed to close tightly around them and bind them in its tentacles. Despair filled the stale air and vibrated through the infinite blackness into their very bones.

CHAPTER 9

✣

*T*he solid clank of cold iron sent a shudder through Louis as the cell door closed behind him. He was in a small cell with two other prisoners. "Welcome to our home," one of the prisoners said sarcastically as he bowed and made a sweeping motion with his hands.

It's not too bad here," the other prisoner added. "We're allowed to go out in the compound for a few hours every day with the other prisoners, get our daily rations then come back to our cells."

"At least they don't beat up on us…yet," said the first.

"You're Acadians?" Louis finally spoke.

"Yes. We were taken prisoner at Fort Beauséjour."

"That's where we wanted to go to join with the French forces." Louis told them.

One of the men in his cell shook his head sadly. "If you had gone to Fort Beauséjour, you would have all been killed. The fort fell to the British. There's no Fort Beauséjour any more. It's now Fort Cumberland."

The other continued, "We were tricked into going to the fort by Colonel Robert Moncton." He stopped and spit in disgust as if trying to cleanse the name from his mouth, then continued. "Between two hundred and four hundred Acadians were placed under arrest. The

French soldiers were made prisoners of war. But we're not even soldiers, we're farmers."

The first spoke again. "We were brought here. Don't know why...but we were brought here. Maybe because we spoke out against the British. All the rest of our people were sent to England."

"Do you have families?" Louis asked.

"We did. Don't know what happened to them. Don't matter. We'll never see them again."

"Why do you say that? What are they going to do to us?" Louis asked.

"Don't know," the man who had spoken first said. "Been here a long time. We'll rot here."

The other man spoke. "Don't complain. At least they let us out in the open air every day, and give us food."

Louis said nothing. Will we be here until we die, he thought?

When they were allowed out of their cells. Louis slowly walked out into the open area. He sat in a corner of the compound, away from where they were handing out the food and drew his legs up to his chest. Alphonse and Jean saw him.

"Aren't you going to get your rations?" Alphonse asked.

"It's my fault we're here," Louis said.

"If we hadn't surrendered, we'd be dead. At least we have a chance to one day go free," Alphonse answered. "Wasn't that your plan?"

"Alphonse, we're going to die here. I just hope it comes soon."

"Don't talk like that, big brother," Jean said as he knelt next to Louis. "It's not like you to talk like that. Here, eat something," he said as he tried to hand Louis a piece of bread.

"No. Just let me die."

"Please," Jean pleaded. "Please don't say that. I need you. You led us through hard times."

"Where have I led you to? Prison? How many have I led to their deaths? Anyway, who made me the leader? Why should I have been the one who led you here?" Louis held his face in his hands. "Emmeline is probably dead. The only way I can find her is to die, too."

Alphonse knelt in front of Louis, grabbed his shoulders and shook him. "Get some sense!" he shouted in Louis' face. We're in this together and we'll get out of this together!"

He pulled Louis' hands away from his face. "Look at me! This is not your fault. It's the British! The damned British! They caused all of this. You had nothing to do with it. Emmeline is not dead!" he shouted. "Do you want to marry my sister?"

Louis didn't answer.

"Do you want to marry my sister?" Alphonse shouted again, their faces inches apart as he shook Louis' shoulders.

"Yes!" Louis shouted back angrily as he shook Alphonse's hands off of him.

"Good." Alphonse stood up and pulled Louis up with him. "Come back to us. Your brother needs you."

Louis felt anger. Anger at Alphonse—anger at letting himself wallow in self–pity—anger at not taking care of his brother. But he felt the most anger at himself for giving up on finding Emmeline alive.

"Brother–in–law," Alphonse said. "You'll find Emmeline and you'll be married. We'll start a new life together with our families. There are new lands that'll welcome us somewhere. Don't give up, brother–in–law. It's not the end. Only the beginning. If we can escape, remember we have guns hidden at our hunting camp."

"Yes," Jean chimed in. "Hey! The three of us…they can't keep us down. We do have a future, and we need you."

The days painfully crawled by, one by one. Louis, Jean and Alphonse made each other follow a daily exercise routine to keep up their strength. One day as they were exercising, some soldiers came into the compound with an officer.

"You Acadians," the officer shouted in French. "You developed the dike system to keep seawater from your farmlands. Our people, the Puritans, are trying to farm, but the spring tides have breached some of the dikes. You are to repair these dikes like you've done in the past. You are to leave tomorrow morning."

The next morning, the Acadians loaded one wagon with shovels and tools then climbed into other wagons for their journey north.

When they arrived at Pisiquid, the Acadians shouldered their shovels and soldiers escorted them to the dikes that protected the fields. The officer in charge told them they would remain there until the work was completed.

As Louis labored, sweat ran down his face. It reminded him of the work he did while clearing land for Emmeline and himself. He felt so lonely. Here was a land, the country of his birth, yet it was no longer his. It was a specter, empty of his people with their familiar customs and language. There was only a memory, like a vapor floating over the lush greenery. He didn't want to repair the dikes. Yet he didn't want to see the precious land destroyed by the salt water.

The work was with his hands, not with his heart. He longed for the green fields of home, his loved ones, and especially his lovely Emmeline. If he had been sent to work at Grand Pré, could he have been able to bear the pain? Would his heart be bleeding in the burned out hulls of familiar buildings and homes or would there be new different structures in their place peopled with strangers? Never again would he see the rows of green corn, the golden fields of grain. Never again would he smell the fresh, clean smell of newly plowed fields and hear familiar laughter of the ones he loved.

But one day he would hold his lovely Emmeline in his arms—hold her tightly against him—run his hands through her soft tresses and smell the perfume of a summer night in her hair. He had to believe this. Life would not be worth living if he didn't.

At night, after eating their meager rations, they would fall on their bedrolls, too tired to talk to each other. After a while, Alphonse even stopped planning ways to escape. Where could they escape to? If they could get to where their guns were hidden, would they still be there or had the Indians or the British found them? Even if they managed to escape and get to their guns, what good would two guns be against an army? Yes, if they escaped without being shot, where could they escape to?

Under the starry sky, Louis wondered if Emmeline was looking at the same stars. He wondered what Emmeline was thinking. Did she miss him as much as he missed her? Sometimes at night when everything was quiet, he seemed to hear her calling him. He recalled her words as he walked away that night. Oh God! Will I ever pass this storm? Will the sun ever shine again?

After weeks of hard labor, the men were finally complete with the repair of the dikes. As they gathered their equipment and prepared to leave, a group of Puritans approached the Acadians. One of them came forward and spoke in broken French; "We want to thank you for what you did to save our land. We know you are criminals because you are prisoners. You sinned against God, or you would not be in prison. God gave us this fertile land because we are faithful. God used you to help us, even though you are sinners."

Alphonse stepped forward and in a loud voice proclaimed, "We are not criminals and sinners!" He slammed his fist into the palm of his hand. "Our only sin is not to bow down before your damned king! This is our land—the land of our fathers! Stolen from us! This is not your land!" He spit in disgust.

A British soldier stepped in front of Alphonse, and with his bayonet prodded him to step back into the group of Acadians.

The man who had spoken to them in broken French turned and said something to the group of other Puritans. He then came back and said, "Accept the punishment that God has given you. He will forgive your trespasses. We are sorry for you. We will pray for you."

This angered Louis. He had to say what he felt. He spoke loudly, "God will reward our people…for the suffering your king has caused. We are the faithful ones. We still have our faith. We don't bow down to your king…only to God."

The soldiers ordered the men to carry their bedrolls and shovels and load the wagons.

As the wagons rolled away, the Puritans fell on their knees in prayer.

The months passed with only the walk in the compound to break the monotony of the cell walls. Each day came and went without time. There was only light and darkness—day and night. Spring became summer because the sun grew hot. Summer became fall because the sun grew dimmer and cool breezes blew. The snow fell and then it was summer again. Their captors cut the food ration in half. They were always hungry. Finally they were only allowed outside of their cells to get their meager rations, then they had to return. If anyone complained, they were beaten.

Louis awoke one morning to a strange sound. He wasn't sure if it was really a sound or a feeling. He sat up and in the dim light of dawn saw a figure hanging from a rafter on the ceiling. He jumped up, realizing that it was a human figure. He yelled and awoke the other cellmate. The two of them got the body down, but it was too late. He was dead.

Louis did not feel any emotions. In fact, he felt that his cellmate was fortunate. He was out of this place. There was no reason to live.

The cold gray walls of the prison cell seemed to close in on Louis. He felt a strong urge to follow his cellmate into oblivion—to numb all the feelings of his body and soul.

In the fog of his consciousness, he heard the clang of his cell door open and thought they had come to remove the body. But then he heard each of the other cells being opened one by one. His dulled mind couldn't comprehend what was happening. Then he heard the commander announce in French, in a loud voice, that they were to gather in the assembly room.

Alphonse found Louis and walked with him. "What do you think?"

Louis didn't answer. He could only think that this was not good. What else could it be but bad news?

The prisoners filed silently into the assembly room. They stood around uneasily until they were told to sit in the chairs. Louis, Alphonse and Jean sat together. Louis wondered why the prison officials were letting them sit in chairs. Were they being nice before the execution? The gaunt group of Acadians was silent—like men waiting for a verdict on their life.

What looked like a French officer strolled in from a side door. Was this really a French officer, thought Louis? Or was this a British impersonating one to make us suffer?

"Good morning," the man said in perfect French. "I am here to bring you good news. The English and French have signed a treaty. You are no longer prisoners."

The prisoners didn't respond. They just sat in silence. It could not be true, what they were hearing. Maybe this was a trick or a cruel joke or maybe they didn't understand what had just been said.

The French officer was silent for a while, then realizing they were in a state of disbelief, said again. "Gentlemen, you are no longer prisoners. I am a French officer and I am here to set you free."

It started as a guttural chuckle, which exploded, into uncontrollable laughter, then into rousing cheers. The men hugged each other with emotional crying and laughter.

"Can this be true?" Louis shouted as he hugged Jean and Alphonse.

"It's true!" Alphonse bellowed. "It's true! We're free!"

The French officer finally called for silence. "You are to leave immediately with me."

There was another round of cheering. Finally when it subsided, he continued. "We are looking for volunteers to help build a French seaport project at Môle St.–Nicolas on the island of Saint–Domingue. Are you willing volunteers?"

"Wait!" Alphonse shouted. "What does this mean? Does it mean the British will leave Acadia?" On hearing this, the Acadians became quiet.

"No," the officer replied. "Acadia is no more. King Louis XV will try to relocate the Acadians."

A moan went up from the men.

"I am here by the order of King Louis XV to free you from prison. He also requests that you volunteer to help the Crown in building a seaport at Môle St.–Nicolas. I ask again. Do you volunteer?"

"Yes," was the muted reply from the prisoners.

What else could they say, thought Louis? Was there another way to get out of here?

"Then you are to gather your personal effects and come with me to the ship which will leave immediately for Saint–Domingue."

As they walked to the ship, Louis commented. "Where is this place they're taking us? No one asked where it was."

"What difference does it make. We're getting out of here. We're free. That means we'll be able to find out where our families are," Jean replied.

"Yes," Louis answered. "Yes, that's true." He finally felt real hope for the first time since he was captured. They would never be able to take back their Country, but there was hope that they would be reunited with their families. King Louis XV knew of their plight. Didn't the officer say the king wanted to relocate the Acadians? This meant that the French would help them find their families. Yes, hope filled his heart—hope that he would find Emmeline—that he would soon be holding her.

The freed Acadians joined others on the ship, who had been freed from British prisons in Boston and New York. They were greeted with shouts of welcome. The ex–prisoners were then fed a real meal.

It had been so song since Louis had tasted good food. He ate until his stomach ached.

When the ship weighed anchor and sailed out of the harbor, Louis, Jean and Alphonse were on deck. No one said a word as they watched their beloved homeland slip below the horizon.

Louis wiped a tear from his eyes, knowing that he would never see his home again. He didn't know what the future held, except that he was free and that he was going to a French colony. The French Crown would surely help them reunite with their families.

When they finally went to their quarters, Alphonse circulated among the other Acadians questioning them at length. After a while, he found Louis and said, "Brother–in–law, no one on this ship knows anything about our families. I asked if anyone knew where the people in the Grand Pré area were sent, other than us. They said they heard some were sent to Virginia, to Carolina, and some were sent to England. But don't worry. We'll find them."

"What do you think we'll be doing at Môle St–Nicolas, and where is it?" Louis asked Alphonse.

"I asked one of the crew," said Jean. "He said it's on an island far to the south. A long way from here. In a sea called the Caribbean, where it's warm all year."

"That's hard to believe," said Alphonse as he pulled off his shirt. "Don't know about all year, but it's getting warm in here right now."

The days passed as the ship cut through long swells of clear, blue water. Louis sat on the deck looking out over this endless blue. He thought about his friend, Fabien. What did his death gain them? Could he have prevented it, somehow? What would he tell Fabien's family?

He was convinced in his mind that all of the Acadians would be sent to Saint–Domingue to settle the island. As the days lazily slipped by and the sun grew warmer, he looked forward to their destination. He felt that this must be the land that God was going to give them. His heart filled with hope.

Louis sat leaning against the superstructure watching the long swells roll by. Every once and a while a small wave would crest and spread white foam on the smooth deep blue surface. He hummed Emmeline and his favorite love song, and imagined holding her in his arms. He could feel her arms clinging around his neck—her soft breasts against his chest—taste her lips pressed against his. He could smell her fragrance—her special fragrance—the fragrance that is unique to each woman.

"What are you thinking about, big brother?" The words startled him from his reverie. He turned to see Jean. "You think we'll find our family at Saint–Domingue?"

"Don't know," Louis answered. "But, I think the King wants to develop that island. He'll see that the Acadians settle a new homeland there. We'll probably meet our families there. Maybe we can call it New Acadia."

"Yes," said Jean enthusiastically with a smile. "Yes. Then you and Emmeline can get married. I'll bet that's what you were thinking."

"How did you know?"

"By that faraway look. Besides, I know my brother very well. I can always tell when you're thinking about her," Jean answered with a twinkle in his eyes.

"It's wonderful to have hope again, isn't it?" Louis said smiling. He stood up and ruffled Jean's hair. "It won't be long, now."

The next morning Louis awakened to a strange sound. He sat up and listened. It wasn't a sound at all. It was the sound of silence. There was not the familiar sound of waves slapping on the bow. The ship sat strangely still. He hurried up on deck. The ship was becalmed. Louis looked out on what appeared to be solid land. Seaweed was floating thickly on the surface of the water as far as he could see in every direction. The sails hung limply.

"What is this? he asked a deck hand.

"This is a calm spot in the ocean. We try to avoid it if we can. We could be here for days," the deck hand proclaimed.

"How do we get out of here?" Louis asked.

"We can only sit here and hope for a breeze to come up," was the reply.

"What's happening?" Alphonse asked as he came out on deck. "What's all this?" He swung his arms in a circle.

Louis wiped the sweat from his face. Already, with not a breath of air moving, the heat was beginning to be unbearable. "We're in a calm," he answered. "Don't know anything else."

As the sun rose higher, it was too hot to stay below, but on deck, the sun seemed to burn right through Louis.

"I got an idea," Alphonse said as he took off his shirt. He found a piece of rope, tied it around his shirt and lowered it over the side. "I'll get it wet and drape it over my head," he said desperately. But when the shirt landed on the thick carpet of seaweed, it just lay on top and wouldn't get wet.

"Well, so much for your idea," Louis chided with a laugh. "But, it would have been good if it worked."

"Damn," mumbled Alphonse. "What kind of a crazy world is this?" He tied some large knots to give weight to his shirt. Instead of lowering it over the side, he held enough slack in the rope to drop to the surface. This time, when the knots hit the seaweed, they punched a hole and allowed his shirt to get wet. "Well, look at this," the elated Alphonse said to Louis as he pulled the dripping shirt up. He squeezed it over his head. "Who's laughing now?"

Louis tried to find a spot in the shade of either the superstructure or a sail. But the deck was too crowded and as the sun moved across the sky, he would lose his shade. Night was the best time because the searing sun did not burn him, but the heat was still unbearable. This went on for three days and nights.

During the third night, a slight breeze blowing across his nearly naked body awakened him. A cheer went up from the ship's crew. Louis heard the sails snap as they filled with wind. Instead of the stale smell of the seaweed, he now breathed in the fresh, salty smell of the ocean.

Lightning flashed in the distance and the ship started to rise and fall. Louis went below when rain started to fall. He slept peacefully through the night.

By morning, the ship was fighting an angry sea. The sails had been trimmed and the order given to batten down the hatches. Louis tried to go on deck, but was told to go back below. A deck hand looked over his shoulders and shouted, "Stay below! Hurricane!"

As he struggled to go below, he heard Alphonse trying to come up. "Go back down," Louis yelled.

"What's going on?" Alphonse asked.

"The hand said hurricane," Louis said above the crash of the waves.

Jean, struggling to stay on his feet, looking like a drunk, came up to the two men. "I've heard of hurricanes. An old seaman once told me they are bad storms that happen in the lower latitudes."

"I've had enough storms," Alphonse said. "Don't want any more."

The rest of the Acadian passengers were starting to worry and complain.

"Calm down and don't panic," bellowed Alphonse above the crashing of the waves over the deck. "Everyone stay where you are or stay in your hammocks, if you can, until the sea calms." He then said in a lower voice, to Louis, "Hope this ship holds together better than those rotten old tubs we had."

The wind screamed in the rigging and the waves smashed against the ship and over her bow. As the hours passed, the wind became a deafening roar and the waves crashed with unrelenting force, sweeping across the deck and against the superstructure. The ship dove and bobbed while the ocean kept its relentless hold, tossing it as a giant playing with a toy.

"Pray!" someone shouted. "Pray we survive the storm!"

Louis began to pray for the storm to end. As he prayed, he seemed to hear Emmeline's voice. He seemed to hear her voice in the roar of the wind and the sea—"Remember my love, beyond the storm the sun is shining."

This is an omen, he thought. We will survive and Saint–Domingue is beyond the storm. That's where Emmeline will be. Even with the roaring and crashing, Louis felt his spirits lifted. I'll soon see my Emmeline, he thought.

Just when it seemed that the ship could not take any more pounding, the storm started to abate.

"Alphonse," Louis said as he crawled to where Alphonse was. "Storm's over. We'll soon be there. I have a feeling Emmeline will be waiting for me."

"Good," Alphonse replied. "We'll be able to have that wedding, brother–in–law. I know our families are there. They'll probably meet us at the dock. Just think of the celebration we're going to have. A good old fashion fun time. We'll make that wedding last a week."

Louis laughed. "Yes, we're going to have that wedding after all."

CHAPTER 10

L and Ho!

The words echoed throughout the ship. A cheer went up from the Acadians. There was a rush to the deck.

Louis looked at the dark line on the horizon. As it got closer he saw green mountains and white beaches. He could smell the perfume of blooming flowers on the warm wind. Along the shore were tall skinny trees with wide, green leaves at the top. He asked a deckhand what kind of trees they were and was told they were palm trees. This is a new world, he thought. Good, he mused. It won't remind me of our Acadia. We can make a new start. The ship dropped anchor in the bay and boats were lowered over the side.

"It won't be long now," Louis said laughing with happiness. "Our families will be on the shore waiting for us."

"Well," Alphonse muttered to no one in particular, "What do you think about this place?"

"I'm anxious to find out more about this new land," Jean said. "This is all new and exciting. And I can't wait to see our families."

"Yes," said Louis. "I think it'll be interesting, learning about our new land with our families. But I don't see a lot of people on the shore. I wonder where the other Acadians are?"

"They should have been waiting for us," Alphonse said. He looked around as the launch approached the shore.

"Maybe they didn't know we were coming," Louis said. He strained to see a familiar face on the shore. "I'm sure we'll meet them after we land…when they find out we're here."

After landing, they were shown to their quarters—two large two-story dormitories. There was a third two-story building that served as offices, a mess hall, a commissary, and a general meeting room on the first floor. The second story served as a sick ward. The three buildings faced each other with a circular assembly area in the middle.

Louis was assigned a bed next to Jean and Alphonse on the first floor. The dormitories had a continuous opened window all around, allowing the breezes to blow through. Mosquito netting was over each bed. A profusion of green, flowering plants surrounded the buildings, giving off a fresh smell mixed with pungent perfume.

After allowing the men to settle down and observe their surroundings, they were told to meet in the meeting room. A French naval officer greeted the men and welcomed then to Môle St–Nicolas. "You Acadians have volunteered to do a service to the king. You will join other Acadians in building a seaport to strengthen the French position in the Caribbean.

"In return for your services, you will be provided with food and shelter. We will pay you for each day that you work. If you become sick, you will be taken care of in our infirmary.

"You may now return to your barracks and not be required to work until tomorrow."

"Where are our families?" Alphonse yelled at the naval officer.

There was no answer. The officer turned and stiffly walked away.

"Why, that bastard," Alphonse turned to Louis. "Who the hell does he think he is?"

That night, after the evening meal, Louis, Jean and Alphonse mingled with the other workers, asking questions.

"Where are the rest of the people? Where are the families? Where are the women and children?" Louis asked one of them.

"There were some families when we first started work here, but the climate wasn't good for the women and children. They got sick with the fever and a lot of them died," the man answered.

"The men collected their pay, what little there was. Took their families to the French Territory of Louisiana," he continued.

"Then, there are only men here?" asked Louis. "No Acadian women in the settlement?"

"No, don't think so," was the answer. "The men didn't want their women to stay here and die so they took them away. Some of us are here because we lost out families to the fever and the rest of us were released from British prisons."

A second man interrupted. "Some of us came from France to get off the dole and make money to have a better life for our families." The man stopped as if thinking then flung his arms out in anger. "Bastards! Even if we made more than slave labor, how could we get it back to them?

Louis didn't want to hear this.

"We're all Acadians here," the man continued. "The king doesn't know what to do with us. He's trying to find places for us."

"What about this place?" Louis inquired.

"This isn't a place for Acadians," another man answered as he sadly shook his head. "Too much heat and bugs. You'll see." He coughed and gagged as he tried to catch his breath.

Another man joined in. "Our people are easy to catch the fever. Infirmary's full. How many of us have died?" he asked as he looked around inquiringly, making a sweep with his arms.

Heads nodding and a series of affirmative grunts answered him.

Louis saw Alphonse walking slowly toward him, head hanging down. What's wrong, he thought.

"Louis, I have bad news," Alphonse said sadly.

"What is it?"

"I…I found out from some of the men…" Alphonse stopped and stood with his mouth opened as if he were choking on words, which wouldn't come out.

"What's wrong, Alphonse?"

"I found out from some of the men…" Alphonse stopped again then slowly forced the words from his mouth. "That…that my father and your father are dead."

Louis couldn't believe what he had just heard. "What…what?"

"Just talked with some of the men from Grand Pré." Alphonse stopped speaking and choked back a sob then continued. "They were on a ship with our fathers. They both died from cholera on board a ship bound for England."

"Are you sure, Alphonse?" Louis felt a wave of cold wash across his body.

"They were there with them," Alphonse said in a whisper as though he didn't want to say it. Then clenching his fists and striking out at an invisible foe, he bellowed out, "Damn the British! Damn! Damn! Damn!"

Louis held his head in his hands. Sobs choked in his throat. Finally, weak from the emotional drain, Louis asked the question he was afraid to ask. "What about our mothers and sisters?" He hesitated. "What about Emmeline?"

Alphonse took a deep breath, then slowly let it out. "Don't know. Some women from Grand Pré were sent to Virginia and Massachusetts. Some were sent to Liverpool, England."

"Then we still don't know where the rest of our families are," Louis said catching his breath.

"No," Alphonse answered as he wiped his eyes. "One thing we know for sure, they're not here."

Louis sighed a deep sigh. Hope for finding his sweetheart and their families was once again wrenched from his grasp. Were any of their loved ones still alive?

"Dear God, help us. What are we to do? We thought this was the paradise you'd give us. It's not. Help us," Louis whispered in despair. "Please help us."

Alphonse put his arm around Louis' shoulders. "Don't worry, brother–in–law. We'll find them. Don't worry it'll be all right."

Jean walked up to them, a confused and worried look on his face. "What's wrong?"

The hot sun beat down on Louis as he and Jean struggled to carry a log to the water's edge to form a bulkhead. Jean stumbled and fell to his knees. "You alright?" Louis asked Jean.

"My knees hurt like hell," Jean answered as he wiped the blood and picked the sand out from his skinned knees. Louis knelt beside him.

Just then, Louis felt a stick hit him on the back. "Pick up that log and get back to work!" the foreman yelled.

Louis jumped up and looked the foreman in the eyes. "We're not prisoners or slaves. We're French citizens. We volunteered to help the Crown. Don't ever touch me or my brother again."

The foreman backed off then turned around cursing under his breath.

"Let's carry this log," Jean said as he stood up.

"Sure you're all right?" Louis asked.

They lifted the log to their shoulders, the rough bark chafed their skin and the sun beat down mercilessly on them. Sweat rolled down Louis' forehead and into his eyes, making it hard for him to see.

"How long do you think we can stand this?" Louis asked Alphonse one night as he wiped the sweat off his face and swatted at a mosquito on the back of his neck.

"Even with the netting on our beds, we still have to fight them off," added Jean. "Don't know how the hell they get in. And another thing, it's hot all the time. The only way we knew it was Christmas was the special meal they served."

"Yes. And the priest had to tell us at mass or…" Alphonse slapped his arm, muttered a low curse, and scratched, then continued, "…or we wouldn't have known. Not like the Christmas we know. But at least we didn't have to work that day."

Christmas, Louis thought. He remembered a Christmas, which seemed so long ago. He and Emmeline had walked hand in hand after midnight mass. The snow crunched under their feet as they looked up into the starry sky. They were filled with joy and peace and love, then.

What is reality? Is it a homeland that is no more or is it this stinking hellhole? Was the promise of the Savior—a promise of peace and love—one that reached all the way here, or did his promise die with our homeland?

He had once asked Fabien if God always answers prayers. Fabien had said, "Always, but not always in your timing. Keep faith in God's promise." How long must I keep faith, Louis thought. How long must I wait?

He was brought out of his thoughts as Alphonse slapped a mosquito that was feasting on his arm.

"Ouch! Let it eat," Louis exclaimed. "It doesn't eat much."

"One wouldn't be too bad," retorted Alphonse. "But ten million?"

"This is almost like slave labor," Louis commented, not speaking to anyone in particular. "We work from dark to dark. It's hard, backbreaking work. But we are making a little money here…" He stopped and was silent for a moment, then continued. "We should have enough by now to buy passage to some place that's not like this hellhole and…"

"And doesn't have these damn bugs," interrupted Alphonse.

"Where could we go?" asked Jean as he took a bite of tobacco he bought from the commissary. "We don't want to go to France. We'd be on the dole there. Besides, we have to find our families."

"You need to stop chewing that stuff," Alphonse said, making a face. "It'll ruin you. I thought Louis taught you better than that."

"Keeps you from getting the fever," Jean said with a mouthful of juice as he walked to the window and spit.

"Won't keep the bugs away," grumbled Alphonse as he slapped at his arm again. "They probably chew the stuff."

Louis rubbed the back of his neck. A large nesting bird, outside of the window, squawked loudly. He itched all over. "Listen. I've heard the men talk of a French territory called Louisiana. There's a city named after one of the cities in France, 'Orleans'. It's on a great river. There's fertile land to be had. They say a lot of Acadians are already there, and many more will be going. I'll bet that's where our families are. Maybe Emmeline is already there waiting for me."

Alphonse grinned. "Hey, lots of Acadian men here are planning on leaving when they can afford passage. That's where they told me they're going."

Jean walked to the window and spit tobacco juice at a green lizard lying on a large flat leaf. "Maybe God is going to give us that new land for what the British took from us. Yes, we might find our families there."

Louis was silent. Deep in thought. Maybe this time…Should he dare to hope? He had had his hopes shattered so many times before. But then, he couldn't live without hope. Maybe this time he could find his love.

"Then it's a plan," Alphonse said with enthusiasm. "As soon as we find a ship bound for Louisiana, we'll book passage."

The three men gripped their hands together in a pledge of unity.

❦   ❦   ❦

It came on suddenly. Louis heard Jean groaning in the bed next to him. "What's the matter?" Louis asked and was answered by more groaning. Louis got up and felt Jean's forehead. He was burning up with fever.

"Wake up." Louis shook Alphonse. "Jean has the fever. Help me take him to the infirmary."

They tried to make Jean stand up, but his knees buckled under him.

"Make a stretcher out of the blanket, and we can carry him," Alphonse said.

At the infirmary, Louis and Alphonse were directed to a bed where they could lay Jean down. The ward was full. In the dim light of the ward, Louis could hear agonizing groans and pleas for water. The sickly smell of death permeated the stale air.

"You'll have to leave," an orderly told them. "He's my brother," Louis answered. "I need to stay with him."

"Go back to your barracks," said the orderly. "He'll be all right. Come back in the morning."

Louis couldn't sleep. He lay on his back with his eyes open, staring into the darkness. *I should never have listened to that orderly. I should have stayed with him. He might need me.*

The hours dragged by. Finally Louis couldn't stand it any longer. He awakened Alphonse. "I'm going to see how Jean is," Louis whispered.

"All right. See you later," Alphonse mumbled sleepily.

Hastily, Louis dressed and hurried to the infirmary. "Look," Louis told the orderly. "I'm here to take care of my brother."

He found Jean tossing and turning. "I'm right here," Louis said as he softly stroked his brother's hair. He asked the orderly for a wet towel, which he laid tenderly on the burning forehead.

"Is there any medication you can give him?" the worried brother asked the orderly.

"With the fever, all you can do is wait it out and hope for the best," was the reply.

Another orderly tapped the shoulder of the one talking to Louis. "Another one died during the night. Need help carrying him out."

Louis wiped his brother's brow with the wet cloth. "You'll be all right, little brother," Louis kept saying. "You'll be all right."

Jean groaned and mumbled, "Water…water…" Louis got a cup of water, and lifting up his head held the cup to his mouth. He choked and the water ran down the side of his mouth.

Louis felt a tap on his shoulder. He looked up to see one of the administrators. "You'll have to go to work. You can't stay here. You have to work."

Louis shot up and looked the man directly in the eyes. "This is my brother. You can't make me leave. We're not slaves."

"You volunteered to work for the Crown," the man insisted.

"That's right," Louis hissed as he grabbed the administrator's shirt. "I volunteered to work for the crown. Today I'm volunteering to stay with my brother. Now get the hell away from me." The man backed off, smoothed his shirt and walked away cursing under his breath. Throughout the day, Louis sat by his brother, wiping his forehead, and now and then soaking a rag and letting him suck the water from it.

After the evening meal, Alphonse stopped by the infirmary and brought Louis something to eat. "Sneaked this out. Thought you might be hungry, brother–in–law. How's he doing?"

"Thanks," Louis answered. "He's not doing well. You know, Alphonse, this climate is not good for Acadians. We're not built for this. As soon as Jean gets well, we'll need to book a ship for Louisiana…as soon as we can."

"I'll go along with that," Alphonse replied. "Want me to stay here with you?"

"Thanks, but I'll be all right," Louis answered, as he bit into the piece of meat and bread that Alphonse brought him.

Through the night, Louis worried. I don't know how much longer he can stand this…the fever has to break soon…his body can't stand much more.

Louis held Jean's hand and talked quietly to him. "You remember when we used to milk the cows together? You were good at squirting milk into the cat's mouth. I never was as good as you. I'd get milk all over the cat's face and she'd walk away shaking her head. Remember when we were kids, the time we snared a wild goose and cooked it over a fire in the woods? It was good, wasn't it? I wonder if there are wild geese in Louisiana. But we're soon going to find out."

Just before dawn, Jean stopped groaning and seemed to slip into peaceful sleep. Good, maybe the fever's breaking, Louis thought. But he felt his forehead and it was still very hot. His breath became labored. "Please don't let him die," Louis said out loud. "He's my brother."

Jean took a slow, deep breath and let it out. The breathing stopped. "No!" Louis cried. "No! Don't go. We have to find our mother."

Louis felt a hand on his shoulder, and then he heard Alphonse's voice. "I couldn't sleep and came by to see how he's doing."

"I think…I think…" Louis sobbed.

Alphonse stood with his hand on Louis. He didn't speak. He just kneaded Louis' shoulder.

An orderly felt Jean's pulse. "He's dead," he said unemotionally.

"No!" Louis cried. "He can't be! He's my brother! We need each other! Alphonse, tell me he's not dead! Jean…" his voice trailed off. A flood of grief welled up from the very depth of his being. As it rose from within him, it tore out pieces of his soul, leaving gaping holes only to be filled by lonely memories of what had been.

Two orderlies came to the bed.

"What are you doing?" Louis choked out the words as he stood up.

"We need to take the body away."

"No! Don't do that! He's not dead! Alphonse, tell them he's not dead!"

Alphonse put his arm around Louis' shoulder. "I'm sorry."

They rolled the body in the sheets. "In the tropics, we have to dispose of the bodies as soon as possible," one of them said.

"Where are you going to bury him?" Louis asked. The words sounded hollow and unreal.

"We burn the bodies to keep the fever from spreading," the larger of the two orderlies replied, as they lifted Jean's body.

"No!" Louis screamed. "Don't burn him!" He ran around to block the orderlies. "Alphonse, help me stop them!"

Alphonse put his arm around Louis and held him back. "They have to."

"Let me go!" Louis screamed. Alphonse held Louis tightly. "They have to," he repeated. "To keep the fever from spreading."

Louis groaned as he watched them carry his brother away. A cold wave of grief washed over and enveloped his body. "Why, Alphonse? Why? Has God forgotten us? First my father, then my brother. Now he can't even have a decent grave. Neither could my father. They fed him to the fishes."

"Maybe not," Alphonse said still holding Louis. "Probably wrapped them in canvas."

"You know they didn't," Louis sobbed. "They just threw our fathers over the side. You think the British cared. Remember what they did on our ship? They just tossed them overboard for the fish to eat. You and I are the only ones of our family and friends who're still alive. They're all dead."

"Don't say that," Alphonse said as he patted Louis on the back. "We don't know. Have faith. Things will turn out all right."

"How?" Louis sobbed. "They're all dead. Maybe the Puritans were right. Maybe God is punishing us. But what have we done to deserve this?"

Alphonse self–consciously cleared his throat then spoke softly, as if his thoughts were far away. "I remember what Fabien once told me. I laughed at him then…" He stopped and was silent as if trying to collect his thoughts. "He said this is not a perfect world, but God didn't make it this way. He gave us freedom to choose good or evil. Our enemies chose evil…God didn't." He stopped, cleared his throat again and continued. "Fabien said to trust in God. He'll make it up to us…either in this world or the next."

"He told me that, too." Louis choked to get the words out.

"Never thought much about what Fabien said before," Alphonse said slowly as he stroked his chin. "I wanted to kill, destroy, make the British suffer for what they did to us. I realize now, that's not the answer." Alphonse was silent for a while, then said with an embarrassed clearing of his throat, "Listen to me." He hit his fist into the palm of his hand and bit his lip. "Damn. What the hell's come over me? I'm turning into Fabien."

He put his arm around Louis' shoulders. "There's still the two of us and I'll stick with you, brother–in–law. We'll get the hell out of here soon as we can."

"I want to collect my pay and my brother's pay," Louis said to the Purser.

"Can't give you your brother's pay. Has to be here in person," he answered as he counted out Louis's money.

"He can't. He's dead."

"Too bad. He forfeits," the Purser answered.

"Look, he earned the money. I'm his brother. I want his pay," Louis countered angrily.

Alphonse pushed Louis out of the way and stepped in front of him. "So, you refuse to give pay for work done? Are you going to keep it for yourself, you bastard?"

"Well…well," stammered the Purser.

Alphonse interrupted him. "I'm sure the Crown would like to hear about this. Do you know what they do to thieves? They execute them. But I'll give you a chance to save yourself. I won't say anything to the Chancellor. I'll make believe this didn't happen if you just give him the money…but now you have to pay a fine…double the pay."

The Purser laughed nervously. "You don't know the Chancellor. How would someone like you know him?"

Alphonse stooped down, placed his hands on the desk and looked the clerk intently in the eyes. "Just try me," he said with ice in his voice. He spoke slowly. His eyes were narrow slits. "How will your neck feel as the rope tightens and you turn blue because you can't breathe? Just try me and find out."

The Purser nervously counted out the money. And put it on the table before him.

"You did not pay the fine," Alphonse slowly said, emphasizing each word. His eyes were like steel cutting through flesh and bone.

The Purser reached into the money sack and counted out more money.

"Now pay me mine," Alphonse said slowly and calmly. The words seemed to hang frozen in the hot humid air. "We're leaving this damned place."

As they walked out of the building, Alphonse smiled at Louis and winked.

CHAPTER 11

"Well, here we are," said Alphonse as they stepped off the ship. Both Louis and Alphonse carried everything they owned in a canvas bag thrown over their shoulders. "Glad to get away from that damned stinking hellhole."

Louis looked around him. People were all around—more people than he had ever seen before. They were scurrying busily here and there. So this is the new Orleans, he thought. How could he find anyone in such a large city with so many people.

An official in uniform escorted them to a large pavilion. There were French soldiers, businessmen and all kinds of official looking people milling around.

They were told to stand in line with many other Acadians to register. The Acadians, some with children clutching to their parents or older siblings, stood in line or milled around. All carried their meager possessions either wrapped in blankets or carried in cloth sacks. This ragtag, threadbare group of lost and confused humanity, who had seen their very existence torn to shreds and scattered to the wind, were still able to smile because they now had hope. They still had a *joie de vie,* a joy of life that could never be taken from them.

"Finally," Louis said to Alphonse after waiting in line for what seemed like an eternity. "We're almost at the table."

"Name," the man at the table said. "Name and where you're from."

"My name is Louis Arsenalt," answered Louis. "I'm from Grand Pré, Acadia."

The man wrote, 'Louis Arceneaux' and following that, 'Acadian French citizen'.

"Wait," Louis exclaimed. "That's not the way I spell my name. How will my family find me if it's spelled wrong?"

The man disregarded Louis' statement. "You will be under the care of the Spanish Crown until we can assign you land."

"Wait," Louis exclaimed again. "Isn't this a French territory?"

The clerk looked disdainfully at Louis and replied, "This territory is now owned by Spain. We're under a caretaker government by France until the Spanish Territorial Governor arrives. Stand over there with the rest of them."

"But what about my name?"

"Move away," the clerk said impatiently. "Next."

Louis felt anger rising. He started to say something to the clerk, but moved to the side. He was afraid that if he caused trouble, they might not let him stay.

Alphonse registered and then he and Louis stood with the group of Acadians who had already registered.

"That damned clerk wouldn't listen," Louis said to Alphonse.

"Let's not cause any trouble," Alphonse cautioned.

Louis looked at Alphonse. "That doesn't sound like you saying, 'Let's not cause trouble.'"

Alphonse laughed.

After everyone in the line had registered, they were ushered to a large building, where they were given food and bedding. "Well, brother–in–law," Alphonse declared. "Another surprise…Spanish instead of French. But I don't care as long as we can stay here." He slapped Louis on the back. "Did you hear? Someone said they'll give us land."

"Sounds too good to be true," Louis answered. "I wonder what's the catch."

Alphonse grinned ear to ear. "There's good people left on earth. Accept it. God is answering our prayers. Maybe this will be our New Acadia."

"Well, I hope so," Louis said. "But, why would they just give us land with no strings attached. There must be a catch." He was quiet for a while, mulling things over in his mind, then continued. "I hope things won't change when the Spanish Governor gets here. I know Spain is our friend, but, you know, I just don't trust governors."

"You can leave your personal things with your bedding and come with me," a uniformed official bellowed. The Acadians were led to a large auditorium where many more people already were.

"Are you Acadians, too?" Alphonse asked as they looked for a seat.

"Yes. We're all Acadians," one of them said. "We came off a ship from France."

Just then a man stepped up onto a raised platform and began speaking in a loud voice: "Welcome, Acadians. The Spanish Crown welcomes all of you. We need settlers to help protect our Territory. You will be given land, a gun, ammunition, and supplies for one year.

"Until we can obtain more gunpowder, we would like for you not to hunt with it. For the time being, it is to be used against the British, if they try to invade the Territory."

"Yes!" the cry went up from the Acadians. "We'll keep the British away."

After the cry subsided, the man on the platform continued: "Our first priority is to develop the land near the city, to supply us with farm products. But there is land available in the Attakapas Indian Country. It is composed of prairie and woodland. We would like to develop a cattle industry there. It is far from any settlement except the Poste des Attakapas to the south. There is water transportation from Poste des Attakapas where cattle can be shipped to our city.

"If you want to be close to the city, you will be given land along the Mississippi River. If you want frontier life, you will be given land in the Attakapas country.

"You can think about it tonight, and tomorrow you can sign–up for the area you would like to settle in."

That night after supper, Louis and Alphonse sat on their bedrolls and talked.

"Well, brother–in–law, what do you want to do?" Alphonse asked.

"I don't know. I've been thinking." Louis stood up and put his hands in his pocket. "I think I'm going to stay in the city."

Alphonse stood up suddenly. "Why?"

"I want to be here to watch and wait for Emmeline."

"Look at me, Louis. You've always been the one with the common sense, but now you're not making any sense. Think about what you're saying."

"Acadians will be coming here. I don't want to miss her."

"You're not making any sense!" Alphonse slammed his fist into his hand.

"I love Emmeline," Louis said, taking his hands out of his pocket and letting them drop at his side. "This may be the only chance I have left to find her."

"Look," said Alphonse as he gripped Louis' shoulders and looked him in the eyes. "I've always let you do the thinking, but this time I'm going to do the thinking. What will you do? Sit here and beg while you watch people file by? She may never come. If you get land, you will make enough money to go out and search for her."

"I want to wait for her. I want to be here when she comes," Louis said rather sharply.

"Louis! Take a deep breath and think about what you're saying. If she does come, do you want her to find you as a beggar? That's not who I want my sister to marry," Alphonse threw his hands up in the air in frustration and let them drop.

"What am I going to do?" Louis rubbed his face with his hands.

"What are you going to do? You're going to get some land and make enough money so you can go out and search for Emmeline...like a man, not a beggar," Alphonse said waving his hands. "You're not thinking straight, Louis."

"Well...maybe you're right."

"You mean you're actually going to follow my advice?" Alphonse said as he laughingly slapped Louis on the back. "Where do you think we ought to settle?"

"But when I get enough money, I'm going to search for her," Louis said.

"If she comes...no, when she comes to New Orleans, she'll see your name in the records and come to you," Alphonse said with a grin. "Now I'll ask again, where do you want to settle?"

"I circulated among the Acadians here asking if anyone knew of our families. No one knew anything," Louis said solemnly. "How will she know where I am? How will she see my name?"

"Let's not give up," Alphonse said. "I went back to the record keeper. He has a book with the names of all the Acadians who came here. I looked through it and didn't find our families. But remember, our names are recorded and our families will be able to find us."

"But, they spelled my name wrong." Louis said as he dropped his hands at his side.

"Well," Alphonse said. "I noticed they spelled a lot of the Acadian names with an 'x'. Don't know why. But they did. Doesn't matter, though, as long as you know who you are. And don't worry, they'll find us." He let out a frustrated whistle.

"Now I'll ask you again and I want an answer. Have you decided where you want to settle?"

Louis looked at Alphonse. "I'd like to go to the Attakapas country, it sounds more like our Acadia than the swampy land near the city. Too much like that hellhole we just came from. What are you going to do?"

Alphonse squinted his eyes and looked hard at Louis. "I told you, brother–in–law, that I'd stick with you. We'll ask for land next to each other." He held his hand out and Louis clasped it.

"You're a good friend," Louis said.

"We're almost like family," Alphonse said as he squeezed Louis' hand. "When you marry my sister, we will be family. Keep acting like this and I'll have to kick the hell out of you." He yawned, stretched and then continued, "Word is out to Acadians all over, that this territory is welcoming them. That's what I heard. So, you see, there'll be more and more Acadians coming here. Also heard a group was coming from Pennsylvania. It won't be long. They'll come here."

"I hope so," was Louis' reply. What would I have done without Alphonse, he thought? He is truly a good friend. Without him to lift my spirit, I don't know if I could have made it.

"Well, let's go into the city," Alphonse said looking around. "Let's see what all these people are doing."

"Let's go," replied Louis.

"First we need to find a good place to eat." Alphonse rubbed his stomach.

They walked down the narrow streets looking in awe at the many people. "Where are they all going?" Louis mused.

"Don't know. Must be important, though. They seem to be in a hurry." Alphonse stopped and looked around. "Maybe they're hungry like me. Let's hurry and find a place to eat." He spotted a restaurant. The aroma of food cooking floated out into the street. "I don't know what they eat, but as long as it's food…" He walked into the door. Louis followed.

"Excuse me, Monsieur." A man dressed like he was a member of a king's court stepped in front of Alphonse. "You can not come in here."

"Why?" Alphonse asked angrily.

Louis' face flushed with anger. "Yes, why can't we come in? We're French citizens."

The man sniffed. "You can not come in dressed as you are."

Louis looked around at the people seated at the tables. The men wore silk shirts and long black coats. The women were dressed in beautiful silk and lace dresses. "Well, this is certainly not Acadia," Louis said out loud.

"The city is not where we'll be," Alphonse scoffed. "Let's go." He turned to go, but not before squinting his eyes at the man and in a loud whisper said, "We'll be back some day."

The man sniffed again and turned his back.

Louis was both ashamed and angry. Who are these people to treat us like this? Aren't we French citizens? Isn't our money good? "Come on Alphonse," he said as he walked out the door and into the narrow street teeming with people. He could hear both French and Spanish being spoken.

Upon seeing their plight, a young man with a woman clinging to his arm stopped and said, "Excuse me, monsieur. But if you are hungry, you can find food at the market. Follow this street and you will come to it. Are you Acadian immigrants?"

"Yes," Louis answered, rubbing his hands on his shabby clothes, seemingly trying to rub the wrinkles out.

"We are Creoles here," the young man continued. "French and Spanish from Europe. You will find our culture different from where you come from. Here, my good man." He reached into his pocket and pulled out a coin. "Get something to eat at the market."

"We have money!" Alphonse blurted out.

"Thank you anyway," Louis said. "We're not beggars." He felt ashamed of his clothes for the first time.

The man put the coin in his pocket. "*Bon chance,*" he said as he walked away. The woman laughed. Louis felt rejected by his own fellow countrymen. Were we not both French citizens?

The sound of a multitude of voices, horses and carriages clattering, footsteps of people passing by, all swirled around him. The perfume of bougainvillea clinging to the courtyard walls filled his nostrils. He peered through wrought iron gates into courtyards at banana trees pressing against porches where people sat talking and fanning. "People live like this?" he said almost to himself. Alphonse also gawked at the sights around him.

Then Louis heard a new sound. As they approached, they saw a strange sight. People with skin as black as night stood on a raised platform. They were in chains! People were buying them! "What is this?" Louis asked Alphonse.

A man standing near heard him. "These are slaves from Africa."

"But...selling human beings?" Louis felt at the same time, surprise, dread and disgust. What if the English had sold us when we were prisoners, he thought? "Why?"

The man answered, "They're just slaves. We need them."

Louis couldn't watch any longer. "Let's get out of here," he told Alphonse. It broke his heart to see the look in their eyes...a look of fear and sadness. And yet through their seemingly broken spirit, in many he could see a proud defiance. "People should be free!" he said. The man heard him and replied angrily, "These are slaves!"

Louis walked sadly away. He knew how it felt to be separated from his family. He knew how it felt to be a prisoner...to lose hope. But to be bought and sold...to be totally without hope...to no longer be considered a human being...only property...he felt sick in his stomach.

The next day, tables were set up in the auditorium. Most of the Acadians asked for land along the river. Louis and Alphonse asked for land adjacent to each other in the Attakapas Country. They were told that a surveyor would accompany them to stake out the land. Each was given a map with their section of land shown on it.

"Look at this, brother–in–law." Alphonse blurted out after looking at the map. "We're right next to each other. And look at the size of our land. We're going to be all right!"

"Attention. All of the people who were assigned to the river land meet here," one man loudly proclaimed. Another man loudly called for the ones who were going to the Attakapas Country to meet with him. He began to speak: "Tomorrow you will be issued a gun and ammunition. We will transport you in a riverboat to Poste des Attakapas. When you arrive, each family will be given rice, wheat, corn and hardtack. You will be given a cow and an ox. You will also be given farm implements and seeds to plant."

He looked around as if to make sure everyone had understood what had been said. This was met with murmurs of appreciation. Then he continued. "Every three months, you will return to Poste des Attakapas to receive three more months of supplies. After one year, you should be self–sufficient. Because there is little danger that the British will be attacking this far from the river, you can use your ammunition to hunt with." The man stopped again, took a deep breath and continued, "We encourage you to raise cattle. You will be given ample opportunity to do so."

"What do you think so far, brother–in–law?" Alphonse commented as he leaned on the railing, watching the rich greenery along the bank slip by as the boat cut through the dark water.

"Well, the British would never get through this swamp and the Spanish have the territory to the west, so I think we'll be safe," answered Louis as he watched a deer bolt through the thick greenery. An alligator slid silently into the water.

"What was that?" Alphonse said through clenched teeth. "Looked like a big lizard. Wonder if they're good to eat? Wouldn't want to tangle with him."

"This is a new land for us," Louis commented as he slapped a mosquito on his neck. "We'll have to learn about it. Wonder what the prairie will be like. Hope they don't have these bugs there."

"Hey!" Alphonse exclaimed as he slapped his arm. "That damned fly bit me! And it hurt!" After a few choice words to the fly, Alphonse was quiet, deep in thought. Then he started whistling a song they used to sing in Acadia. It was the first time Louis had heard him so happy since the exile.

"Hope the Indians will be friendly," Louis said half to himself. "We have a lot to learn from them about our new land."

His thoughts drifted back to the Indians who had befriended them and saved their lives during that long winter. I hope we're not taking their land. He promised himself that he would not drive any Indians from his land. He would treat them as brothers and learn from them.

The lush vegetation opened up and he saw large plantations along the bank. They soon came to a wooden dock, busy with activity.

"Well, this is our new home," Louis said as the boat tied up.

"Can't wait to get my feet on the ground," Alphonse said. "You can tell a lot about a place by the feel of the ground under your feet."

"How did that stinking hellhole in the jungle feel under your feet?" Louis asked jokingly.

"I knew as soon as my feet touched ground that it wasn't a good place."

Louis laughed. "I hope your feet tell you something good about our new home."

"Well, brother–in–law," Alphonse said as he raised one foot and pointed it toward the shore. "I can feel it from here and it feels good." He let out a hearty guffaw.

"Grab your bedroll," Louis said. They're already starting down the gangplank."

"Come on, brother–in–law! Let's greet our new home!" Alphonse let out a hoop.

The Acadians filed off the boat and wandered bewilderedly on the dock waiting for someone to tell them what to do. Townspeople came to gawk at the ragtag group that was getting off the boat. Children ran alongside them laughing and making fun of the clothes they wore.

Someone told them to go to a public area in front of the church. A short man in a large, wide brimmed hat met them.

"Attention, Acadian immigrants," he bellowed loudly. "I am the surveyor. Your land has been surveyed and staked out. On the edge of town you will be given provisions, a cow, an ox and a plow. You will load your provisions and plow on the ox. There are some wagons for sale by the townspeople if any of you have money. We will leave from here in one hour. My assistants who are familiar with the grants will accompany you and show you your land." He smiled smugly and looked around. "Good luck and God bless." The man touched the brim of his hat then strode off down the street.

"Let's pool our money and see if we have enough to buy a wagon or a cart," Alphonse said, rubbing his hands together.

"All right," answered Louis.

"Then let's go," Alphonse said eagerly.

"You go," Louis said as he looked around him. "You're a good negotiator and it only takes one. There's something I want to do."

"Suits me. I'll show you what kind of a negotiator I am," Alphonse proclaimed.

After Alphonse left, Louis joined several who entered the church to give thanks. The church was cool and peaceful. It smelled of incense and candle wax. "Please God," he said under his breath as he knelt at the altar rail. "Please let me find Emmeline. Let me share my new life with her."

When Alphonse came back, he was grinning from ear to ear. "Don't say I'm not a negotiator. With the money we had, I got not only a wagon, but a horse, too. Don't have a saddle, but a bridle came with the horse."

"Why a horse?" Louis asked in surprise. "The ox can pull the wagon."

"You won't believe this," Alphonse proudly announced. "But I met a man. Don't remember his name, but I'll know his face. He said after we're settled on our land, he'll come by to see us. He has a contract for us to sign. He'll leave several head of cattle with us. Every year after that, he'll visit us. Half the new calves will be his, and we can keep the other half. That way we can build up our herd. But he said we'd need a horse. So I got us a horse."

"How long is this contract for?" asked Louis.

"Five years," Alphonse responded happily. "He'll buy whatever we want to sell him from our half. After five years they'll all be ours and he'll still buy from us. How can we lose on a deal like that?"

"Well, it looks like we're gonna raise cattle." Louis grinned with anticipation. "Let's get started."

Louis couldn't believe what he saw. His land was a combination of grassland with scattered groups of trees that looked like islands on a sea. The breezes bore the perfume of wild flowers. The prairie was a flat plane to the west but as he faced east, the plane came to an abrupt halt and sloped downward to a bayou and thick woods below. It reminded him of his and Emmeline's Beaubassin in his beloved Acadia.

His thoughts brought him back to a time, which seemed so long ago, when he and his sweetheart stood holding hands looking down at their Beaubassin. I'll build a house right here, where we can sit on the porch on summer evenings. This will be our new Beaubassin.

He tried to remember how it felt to hold her in his arms, her brown curls flowing down her back—the smell of her fragrance. It was getting harder and harder to remember—like a dream fading…fading.

God has given me back my Beaubassin, he thought. I know He will give me back my Emmeline. I'll build another place to share our love right here. The house and I will wait for her at our Beaubassin.

"Where do you want to build your house, brother–in–law?" Alphonse's voice interrupted his thoughts.

"Right here where I'm standing," answered Louis.

"Looks like a good place," Alphonse said, rubbing his hands together. "We'll build your house first, then my house within sight of yours. We'll build it just like in Acadia. The steep roof will shed the heavy rain, not the snow. We'll build them big enough for a family, because we're both going to get married and raise families."

"You know what?" Louis said as he turned all around making a sweeping gesture with his arms. "This is the New Acadia. Maybe there'll be an Acadian village near here. Other Acadians will come. Some day this will be a prosperous land filled with happy people, safe from tyrants. This is our land. God has given us back our Acadia."

CHAPTER 12

❀

*A*lphonse helped Louis build his house. Louis knew exactly how he wanted it and each detail had to be perfect in anticipation of when Emmeline would be with him. Louis helped Alphonse build his, but it was an easier job because Alphonse was not as particular.

Like white clouds on a summer day, the years slowly drifted by. The two friends worked together on their ranches, combining their efforts, and soon each had a sizable herd of cattle. A small village sprang up a few miles away. The Acadians in the area met there on Saturday night to sing and dance. This was where the young men met the girls. On Sunday they would go to mass at the church.

Alphonse met an Acadian girl and married. They had two little children, a boy and a girl. Louis adored them. He was "Uncle Louis."

Sometimes, in the evening, Alphonse would visit Louis. They would talk about the weather, maybe play cards, and occasionally plan how they would help each other with a difficult project.

One summer evening, Louis sat alone on his porch, looking out over Beaubassin, watching the last light of the fading day disappear. Fireflies flickered like twinkling stars. A warm breeze softly caressed his face bringing with it the perfume of honeysuckle. A large night flying moth flitted by.

Louis was lonesome. So lonesome that he felt hollow inside. Like an empty shell. What good is all this without a love to share it with?

He wanted to share it with Emmeline. If only he could. Through the years, his love for Emmeline was still there, deep in his heart. But the dream was fading. He didn't want it to. He wanted to keep this love fresh in his mind, but how long could he?

"Hey! Louis!" The sound of Alphonse's voice startled Louis. "Thought you might not be home. Didn't see a lamp lit."

"I was just sitting here thinking," Louis said quietly.

"That's the problem with you. You sit around and think too much. If you had a couple of kids, you wouldn't have time to think," Alphonse said loudly. "You need a woman."

Alphonse stopped as if to let his words sink in, then continued. "I know. I know. But you can't wait your whole life for Emmeline. I want more than anything for you to marry my sister..." Alphonse paused for a long time then said softly. "As much as I don't want to think about it...let's face it...our families are probably dead. Look at all the sickness, and hardship, and death we've seen." Alphonse pulled up a chair and sat in front of Louis, looking into his friend's face.

Louis spoke softly almost under his breath. "Why do you want me to forget Emmeline?"

"No. Don't forget her. You'll always have her memory. But sometimes we have to let go of a dream to be able to go on—to live."

"You know," Louis said slowly, as if reliving a memory. "The last time I kissed Emmeline, she told me that beyond the storm the sun still shines. We've gone through the storm. Where is the sun?"

Alphonse moved closer to Louis, looking intently into his face. The moon was coming up over the Basin, filling the shadows on the porch with its soft glow. "I have my sunshine. It's time you have yours. My wife knows a young woman named Joan who would be good for you. She's pretty. She's healthy. And she wants to get married. She could help you and you could raise a family. Look to the future, my friend. The storm is behind you. The sunshine is before you."

Louis closed his eyes, took a deep breath and slowly let it out with a sigh. "I guess you're right. Maybe I can make someone else's life happy. Pining away for Emmeline is just wasting a life. All right, introduce me to her, Saturday night."

The next morning, Louis arose before dawn, ate breakfast and mounted his horse to check on the cattle. Some wolves had been seen in the area and he didn't want a newborn calf taken.

The sun was just beginning to cast a pink glow on the sea of grass. In the distance he saw a group of cattle just starting to move around in the dim light. The morning dew freshened and cooled the air. Just then he heard a bellow that sounded like a calf in trouble. A wolf, he thought and spurred his horse to a gallop.

As he approached, he saw a dead calf lying on the ground and a figure running toward a group of trees. He cut around it to head it away from the shelter of the trees, as he pulled his pistol. In the dim morning light, he saw that the figure was that of a man carrying a bow. Louis shot his pistol in the air and the man stopped and fell to his knees.

Louis dismounted and walked to where the man was. He could see him clearly now—an Indian. With sign language, Louis told him to stand up.

The Acadian asked the Indian with signing, "Why did you kill my calf?"

The Indian signed, "Our land was taken from us by the White Man. We travel many days toward the setting sun. We try to reach our brothers, who have gone before us. I am with my family. We have old people and babies. My family is very hungry. I kill to eat. Please let me go to my family. Do not kill me."

Louis thought about the Indians who had befriended him and the others—who had saved their lives. Wasn't the plight of these poor Indians very much like the Acadians?

"Where are you going?"

"We are looking for a land where we can hunt and live our lives in peace," the Indian answered.

Louis felt a familiar pain. "Where are the people who are with you?"

The Indian motioned toward the small stand of trees.

"Take the calf," Louis signed. "Stay as long as you like, my brother. You may make a fire to cook your meat without fear. Take what you need while you are here. That house is where I live." Louis pointed toward his house. "There is a well with good water. You are welcome to drink and fill your water bags. I will put out some corn for you."

The Indian smiled at Louis. "You are a good man. The Great Spirit will give you happiness. Why are you doing this for Indians? You are a White Man."

"We are all brothers," Louis answered. "I am repaying a debt. Stay as long as you like and when you leave, take what you need for your journey. Go toward the setting sun, my brother. Maybe you will find a land made for you. You will find your People there. May the Great Spirit be with you."

❋   ❋   ❋

Saturday night was a festive occasion for no other reason but that it was Saturday night. The young people came to dance and laugh. The old people came to watch and smile. Everyone came, parents, babies, children and teenagers. Music from the accordions and fiddles filled the building. Everyone brought something to slake their thirst between dances—cider, wine, ale, water.

"Louis, I want you to meet Joan." He heard Alphonse's voice above the music and laughter.

The shapely young woman had long, black hair and dark blue eyes. She smiled. He stood up and took her hand. It had been so long since he held a girl in his arms.

"You dance so well," Joan whispered.

"I haven't danced in a long time," Louis answered.

They danced as long as the music played and stopped only to drink from a jug of her father's wine to wet their dry throats. "You'd better slow down," Louis cautioned Joan after seeing her drink quite a bit of wine. "Don't worry," she said. "My father's wine is not strong and I am really thirsty."

Before the dance was over, Louis was out of breath. "I'm sorry. I'm not in practice. Let's not dance anymore."

"You need more practice," Joan said with a laugh.

"Would you like for me to take you home?" Louis asked.

"You'll have to ask my father."

Joan's father was hesitant, but gave Louis permission.

Louis noticed that Joan was a little unsteady on her feet and he had to help her climb up on the buckboard. The wagon bounced and swayed and Joan moved closer to him.

"I've had a little too much wine," Joan said. "The road's so rough. Could I hold you around the waist? I'm afraid I might fall off."

"I was afraid that you might have had a little too much," Louis said, but was glad to oblige.

"Why are you not married?" she asked.

"Well, you see," Louis answered. "There was a girl back in Acadia."

"Where is she now?"

"I don't know. I've waited and prayed and watched, hoping we'd meet again, but…" his voice trailed off.

"Then, you're all alone in that big house?" She shook the hair from her face. "You need someone to take care of the house…to cook and care for you."

Joan took her arm from around his waist to use both hands to push back her hair. At that moment the wagon hit a rut. She fell toward him and her hand landed on his leg. It remained there for a long moment as if trying to regain her balance. "Oh, I'm so sorry," the young woman said softly as she looked up into his eyes. They continued on without either saying a word.

After a long period, Joan broke the silence. "That big house is going to waste," she laughed.

"Why do you say that?"

"Well, just you alone in that big house." She laughed again. "You need to get married," she continued. "That house needs to be filled with children's laughter."

"You know, you're right," Louis said softly. "That house is so empty…" His voice trailed off. They were silent for the rest of the trip.

"Well, you're home," Louis said as he pulled back on the reins and the wagon stopped.

He put his hands around her waist and helped her off the wagon. After her feet were on the ground, he stood for a while, holding his hands against her body, feeling her body move with each breath. Moonlight made her white skin seem to glow. She pulled her hair up off her neck then let it fall loosely on her shoulders. She looked up into his eyes. Soft hands touched his chest and slowly slid up until her arms were around his neck. Their lips met. Louis felt a warm, hungry feeling fill his body. Hungrily he kissed her neck, sliding his hands along the curve of her hips. He pulled her tightly against him. The young woman pushed away. They were both breathing hard.

"Stop," she whispered breathlessly. "Not yet."

They stood silently looking at each other. "When will I see you again?" she whispered.

"I'll come for you next Saturday," he answered.

As Louis rode home, his thoughts wandered. It would be nice to have a woman in his house. But what about love? Could he ever love this woman? He knew that it was just physical now. She was a beautiful woman. Maybe he could learn to love her in time. Frontier life was hard and he needed someone. Was love really necessary?

Something tugged at his heart and he was filled with guilt. Had he given up on Emmeline? But then what if she were dead? Should he waste his life waiting for a dream? Louis was torn between the here and now, and a dream—a hope—that he could not let go of.

Louis awakened early and went to the hen house to get some eggs for breakfast. As he opened the back door, he saw something on the steps. He picked it up and looked at it. It's a dream catcher, he thought. Left by the Indians. They believe that it will catch your dreams and make them come true.

Louis looked toward the group of trees. He didn't see the curl of smoke that he had seen every morning from their campfire. He mounted his horse and rode toward the little island of trees. When he arrived where the Indians had been camping, he dismounted and looked around. There was no sign that anyone had ever been there, not even a burned place where the campfire had been. The only thing left behind was the mist of a memory.

It was a hot sultry afternoon. Louis had gone back to the house to get out of the broiling sun and to get a drink of cool water when he heard the sound of a wagon approaching. Straining his eyes, he saw that it was Joan.

As she climbed down from the wagon, she took her bonnet off, and let her long, black hair cascade down her back. She is a beautiful woman, Louis thought as she came up the walk. He stood on the porch waiting for her. She greeted him with a smile.

"Can I talk to you?" Joan asked as she pushed her hair from her face.

"Sure," answered Louis. "Would you like to come in?"

"No," Joan said. She was silent for a while. "I want to apologize for Saturday night," she continued. She shuffled her feet nervously.

"You have nothing to apologize for," Louis said, holding his hands out.

Instead of taking his hands, she stepped backward. "Please hear me out," she stuttered nervously. "I'm not like that. I had a little too much of my father's wine."

"It's all right," he said.

"Ever since I first saw you, I've wanted to know you. I wanted you to be in love with me. That's why I acted that way. I'm sorry," she mumbled, looking down on the floor. Then she slowly raised her head and looked up at him. Her eyes were pools of liquid blue. "I would make you a good wife," she continued. "I could make you happy. I would never refuse you anything. I would take care of you. I can cook, clean the house, wash your clothes…" She stopped to catch her breath. "You could learn to love me."

Her long, black tresses lay on the curve of her breasts. Her white skin was without blemish. His eyes moved down to her heaving breasts—the curve of her hips. She was very young, entering the flower of her youth.

As he looked at her, his breath became quicker. He wanted to carry this young woman to his bed, strip her clothes off, bury his face in those soft breasts, feel her smooth skin, and hungrily kiss those red lips…he forced his imagination to stop at this point. He didn't love this woman. He wanted her so she could fill his physical needs. Could he learn to love her? Would she be able to satisfy his emotional and spiritual needs as well as his physical needs?

This was frontier life. He needed a woman to help him. She was healthy and beautiful. What else could he want? They could have children to help with the chores. Maybe he should marry this woman. Does it have to be for love? We would be there for each other. We would be faithful to each other.

As he looked at Joan, he could see Emmeline's face. No. His heart was still too full of love for Emmeline. While he would be making love to this woman, he would be thinking of Emmeline. He would be holding her soft, warm body, and it wouldn't be hers. It would be Emmeline's.

"Joan," he began hesitantly. "I think you're a lovely woman. I think you'd be a good wife and mother to our children…"

"Then," she interrupted eagerly. "Then, you'll marry me?"

"Joan," Louis said, looking into her eager eyes. "Joan…" He took a deep breath and breathed a sigh. "It wouldn't be fair to you. I'd want you only for what you could do for me. I couldn't give you what you really want. I couldn't give you the love you deserve and need."

"You would learn to love me," she pleaded. "I want to give to you. You don't have to return anything but your faithfulness."

"I would be faithful. That's true," Louis said softly as he clenched and unclenched his fists. "But I couldn't really love you." His mouth was dry and he had to swallow repeatedly. "I couldn't give you my soul. It belongs to someone else."

Her eyes, moist with tears, looked up into his eyes. He had the feeling she was looking into his soul. She spoke in a soft whisper. "I know that after…that after…you wouldn't want anyone but me."

"Please." The words came out of Louis' mouth. He didn't want them to, but they came out. "We both know this isn't the way we want it to be." He was silent for a long time, looking into her eyes. "Maybe someday I could love you…But don't wait for me. Find someone who will freely return your love."

Tears welled up in her eyes. Louis wanted to hold her tightly against him—to kiss the tears from her eyes, but he couldn't. He placed his hands on her shoulders, let them slide down her arms then drop at his side. A tear rolled down her cheek. She wiped her eyes, turned and walked out of his life. Was he making a mistake? Should he take this woman into his life? He started to call her back but the words wouldn't leave his mouth.

He watched as she climbed onto the buckboard. A lonely, hollow gnawing gripped at him as the wagon disappeared in the distance…only dust drifting in the wind.

"I love you, Emmeline," he said in a hoarse whisper. "Oh God how I want you. Dear God, please bring my beloved to me."

CHAPTER 13

"So, you're ready for the cattle drive to the market at Saint Martinsville?" Alphonse asked Louis as he relished the last bite of cornbread. He smiled and looked up at his wife. "You don't know what you're missing not having a woman to fix breakfast for you." He wiped his mouth. "Are you sure you can handle both our herds?"

"Sure," answered Louis as he sipped a cup of hot milk. "Stay with your wife and children. It'll take a week to herd the cattle, sell them and return. I'll hire a couple of boys from the village to help. Just see about my place while I'm gone."

Just then the youngest of Alphonse's children, a little girl with a head full of ringlets, came toddling into the room. Upon seeing Louis, she ran to him with her arms raised for him to pick her up. "Uncle Louis," she chirped. Louis picked her up and gave her a hug. He longed to have children of his own. If things had been different…but then he needn't harp on that.

"Look," Louis said to Alphonse as he leaned across the table. "I want you to know that when I come back from the cattle drive, I'm going to leave to search for Emmeline."

"What?" Alphonse gasped. "Where will you go?"

"I don't know. But I can't sit here and wait. I have to go."

"What about your land?"

"Take care of it while I'm gone. My land means nothing to me without Emmeline. If I don't come back, it's yours."

"Louis. Don't do that. You don't know where to go."

"Alphonse...you've been a good friend. I love you just as if you were my brother. But I can't live without Emmeline. My soul is empty. My life is without purpose."

"Louis, I beg you, don't do this. We'll miss you."

"Uncle Louis, don't go away," the little one said as she hugged Louis around his neck.

"Sweetheart," Louis said as he kissed her innocent face. "Your uncle Louis will come back and he'll bring back someone you'll love, your aunt Emmeline."

The cattle drive was uneventful. Louis received a good price and paid the boys who had helped him with the drive. He then went into a saloon for a well–deserved drink.

While talking with the men in the saloon, he was told that there was a riverboat arriving in two days with some Acadians settlers on board. Louis had met Acadian settlers from the riverboat in the past, hoping that someone might know something about Emmeline or his family—that maybe Emmeline might even be on the boat. But each time, his hopes had been dashed. Should he wait? He felt that it would be futile. But, being that he was here...What were two more days? There was always that remote possibility that maybe this time...

Louis walked down the street to an inn and inquired about a room. After he had made arrangements, he strode down the main street looking into the various shops. Yes, they call this *"Petit Paris",* he mused, looking at all the Paris fashions. His thoughts drifted back to the fine silk shirts the men wore in that restaurant on his first day in Louisiana. They wouldn't let him in then, dressed in the worn and tattered clothes he had arrived in. He could afford a fine silk shirt now. How would it feel against his skin, he thought? Louis entered a shop and felt the fabric of a soft white shirt.

"Can I help you monsieur?" a woman asked, looking at Louis' course, homespun cotton shirt.

Louis at once felt both proud and ashamed. Proud that could now afford such finery and ashamed that he would even think of buying something as frivolous as this. "Thank you. I was just looking," he said. The woman smiled disdainfully. Louis left the shop.

Trying to while away the time, Louis spent the next day walking along the banks of Bayou Teche. Spanish moss draped in long, gray tresses from the live oak trees. Flowers bloomed in profusion along the bayou and in the yards of the houses. Their perfume filled the air. The dark brown water of the bayou silently slid by. Now and then a fish jumped, breaking the mirror–smooth surface.

As he walked, he found himself in front of the church. The door was opened as if inviting him in. It was cool and peaceful inside. He sat in one of the pews. It was as if he were surrounded with peace and love—a lonely man. He sat absorbing it, letting his soul rest—wanting to purge this loneliness from his heart—praying that this emptiness, this void, would be filled.

In the evening, he sat on the veranda of the boarding house and watched couples walk hand in hand in the dim glow of the street lamps. The warm night air carried on it the delicate essence of magnolias. Now and then he could hear the muffled laughter of lovers as they shared intimate secrets. Would he ever be able to love again, he thought? Should he give up his dream of ever finding Emmeline? Could he?

The day that the riverboat was to arrive, Louis stayed near the docks. He tried not to hope, afraid that disappointment would tear at his heart. He didn't want to risk it, but try as he might, hope kept rising in his heart.

He wondered about the Acadians who were coming. Where had they been since the exile? Were they coming to start a better life?

Were they coming to meet family who had gone ahead, or were they looking for someone—a loved one who had been separated from them—lost in the infinite vastness of the land and the sea? It was a vastness that Louis couldn't comprehend. Distance was measured in terms of weeks, months, years.

Would Emmeline be on the boat? Why should she? Several times he started to leave, yet each time something seemed to pull him back. The spark of hope that he tried to suppress became like a seed buried beneath the frozen earth of winter, trying to push toward the promised warmth of spring in the hope of becoming a beautiful flower. The longer he waited the stronger it became. Emmeline was on that boat! He knew it! It was as if she were calling out to him. A new-found joy enveloped him. Louis knew that she must be getting closer and closer! He could feel it!

What was that? Was that a boat whistle? There it was again! Yes! Louis saw the boat coming around the bend in the bayou! Smoke poured from the stack. The paddlewheel churned the water. Again the whistle sounded! It had to be carrying his love! Somewhere inside was his Emmeline! The love that he had waited so long for! His heart beat faster as the boat tied up on the dock.

How many times had he done this? Only to be crushed with disappointment. But he had never had this feeling before. He felt as though his prayers had finally been answered! Louis waited with expectation for the passengers to disembark.

Why did he continue to set himself up for disappointment? But then, it would be different this time. This time she would be on the boat. He tried to remember how it felt to hold her in his arms. It was all so long ago…another world…another life. All these years of waiting were about to end. He could start living again! His lonely nights would soon be over! Hurry my love! Hurry!

The first to file off the boat were ladies in elegant Paris fashions, carrying parasols and hanging onto the arms of well–dressed gentle-men. These are not immigrants, Louis thought. Where are the Acadians? Was this all? He waited, and feeling dejected, was about to leave when he saw another group of more modestly dressed people file from the deck and down the gangplank. His heart leaped. These must be the Acadians. Was she with them?

"Are you Acadian?" he asked the first of the group as they stepped off of the gangplank.

"Yes," came the reply.

A group of twenty or so people gathered around him. The men were carrying their belongings in sacks. Women carried their babies in their arms or on their hips.

"Welcome to New Acadia," Louis said. This was met with smiles. "Is this all of you?" he asked anxiously looking around.

"Someone is supposed to meet us here. Who are you?" a man in a homespun gray shirt asked.

"I'm an Acadian like you. I heard that a boat with Acadians was coming," Louis replied. "Are there more of you?" he again asked.

"Someone is supposed to meet us here," a woman said as she adjusted her child on her hip. "To bring us where our relatives live."

"Where are you from?" Louis asked.

"We were in Virginia when we heard about Louisiana," a white haired man answered. "From our relatives who live here."

"I was hoping that someone I knew would be with you. Do you know anything about…"

The bellowing of a large stocky man as he walked toward the group drowned Louis out. "*Cousin! Mon Ami!*" Shouts and hugs greeted him. The group left the dock following the relative.

Louis watched them leave. He turned toward the boat, hoping to see a familiar figure walk down the gangplank. He knew that there was little chance that Emmeline would be on board…the Acadians had all gone. A flood of disappointment now extinguished the spark of hope that had flickered and almost burst into flame. Why had he allowed himself to do this—to feel this joy, only to be crushed? What made him think that Emmeline would be here? Why would today be different? He was overwhelmed with despair. Loneliness tore a hollow cavern in his soul. There is no more lonely feeling than when hoping to see someone you love emerge from a portal, you look and wait in vain—only emptiness.

After a long empty wait, Louis turned and slowly walked away. Bitter tears of disappointment ran down his cheeks. He didn't want to face another lonely day. Why should he live? "Why God, do you let me live? Please take me. Let me die." What was there to live for? Lonely emptiness without hope?

"Louis?"

He stopped.

"Louis?" He heard it again. That voice. Was he imagining? Could it be? Would he turn and have his hopes crushed again? No, he just thought that he had heard it. A lonely, disappointed mind can play tricks on you. He started to walk away, but then…he slowly turned, afraid of what he would not see. A woman stood on the gangplank. Brown curls cascading loosely on her shoulders.

"Emmeline?" gasped Louis.

"Louis!"

"Emmeline!" he shouted.

She ran off the gangplank and onto the dock. He ran down the dock toward her. They met and he scooped her up in his arms.

"Oh, Louis! I thought you…" Her words were silenced as Louis covered her mouth with kisses. Unashamed, they embraced—enveloped in a mantle of love—two lovers alone in paradise.

Some of the elegant couples who were waiting for carriages looked on and smiled patronizingly.

Louis bought a buggy for the long ride back. He had come on a horse but he told Emmeline that this was now her "royal carriage". They sat closely together. Every now and then, one or the other would initiate a hug, which would end in a long, passionate kiss.

"Oh, Louis. I was so afraid that you were married."

Louis looked at Emmeline. "How could I?"

They silently sat absorbing each other's presence. Finally Louis spoke. "Tell me about yourself," he said as he shook the reins. "What happened after you left Acadia? What about our mothers and sisters?"

"I was separated," she said. Her eyes filled with tears. She became quiet. Her breath came in slow deep sighs. Louis heard her sob softly and turned to look at her. "I'm so sorry."

At the sound of his voice, she sobbed openly.

He drew her tightly to him and held her. Finally when the sobbing stopped she continued. "I don't know what happened to anybody." Emmeline took a handkerchief from her handbag and wiped her eyes. She hesitated, and then as if afraid of the answer she might hear asked almost under her breath. "I saw Alphonse's name...is he...is he...?"

"Yes, Alphonse is here."

Emmeline clutched his arm. "Thank God! My brother is alive and here. Is he well?"

"Very much so. He's married and has two children." Louis laughed.

A smile brightened Emmeline's face, but then she became solemn. "Is there...is there any more family?"

"No...there was Jean...he died of the fever."

"I'm so sorry," Emmeline said.

Louis pulled back on the reins and the buggy stopped. "What is it?" Emmeline asked.

Louis turned and looked at her. "I have some bad news to tell you."

"What is it?" She repeated.

"We were told that both of our fathers died on a ship to England."

"Oh, no! Are you sure?"

"That's what someone told us."

"Then you're not certain. Maybe it's not true. Maybe they were wrong."

They held each other. She cried softly for a while, then sat up, took out a handkerchief and wiped her eyes. "There's always hope…until we know for sure…"

"Yes, my darling," Louis said softly. "We have to hope."

They rode in silence, both deep in thought. Then Emmeline reached out for his hand. "I'm so happy to find you," she said cheerfully.

"Tell me, where did you go after you…after you…?" Louis asked.

She hesitated, looking off in the distance. "It seems so long ago…just women and children on our ship. I can still hear the children crying." She stopped and was silent. Then she heaved a long sigh, wiped her eyes again and continued. "We were closed below deck in the dark, with just the light from the open hatch. They let us off in Virginia. None of the townspeople wanted us around.

"I was taken in by a kind family and became their servant for room and board. The only time I had off was to go to church on Sunday, but at least I had food and shelter."

She squeezed his hand and looked up into his face and continued. "I met an Acadian family at church. They told me that Acadians were going to Louisiana. The Spanish wanted them there and were giving land grants. They said they were going. I asked if I could go with them. They agreed.

"The family I was working for didn't like it, but they let me go. They even gave me money." She was silent for a long time, then she looked at him and laughed. "I found your name in the records in New Orleans. At least I hoped it was your name. They had spelled your name with an 'x' on the end. That's why I came here hoping it was you." She gave his hand a squeeze. "But, you're here. That's all that matters."

Louis smiled. He felt as though he could truly live again. "We won't tell Alphonse you're here 'till tomorrow," Louis said as he shook the reins and clicked his tongue. "Tonight is for us." She looked at him and smiled.

The last rays of the dying sun were fading as they approached the house. "What do you think?" Louis asked proudly.

"Oh! I love it!" Her voice trailed off. "It looks like the houses back in Acadia."

Louis pulled Emmeline close to him. "I built it with you in mind. It's been waiting for you. The house and I knew you would come some day." He kissed her softly and slowly, savoring the taste of her lips. Then he helped her down from the buggy.

"Close your eyes and come with me," he said as he took her by the hand. "Now don't peek until I tell you." He led her up the steps onto the porch and turned her to where she could see the land sloping down to the woods along the bayou. A full moon had risen and covered the world with a magical blanket of pale moonlight, turning the landscape into a surreal dreamscape. "All right. Open your eyes. This is our Beaubassin," he added softly.

She stood speechless.

"This is the dream that was taken from us," Louis continued softly as he swept her hair back and kissed her neck.

"Oh Louis," she whispered. "It's finally come true."

"The Indians gave me a dream catcher, it must have caught our dreams." He slowly ran his fingers through her curls.

The moon splashed its silver on the spanish moss hanging from the live oak trees. Its soft glow reflected in her hair. The perfume of night blooming flowers drifted on the warm breeze. An owl hooted in the distance. Moonlight softly outlined the features of her face. They looked into each other's eyes.

"I've waited so long," Louis said softly. "My love never faded. I'll always love you."

"Oh, Louis," Emmeline whispered. Tears filled her eyes.

"Tomorrow," Louis said. "We'll go into the village and ask the priest to marry us, for the record. But tonight, in the eyes of God, we're already married."

Emmeline reached her arms around his neck and their lips met in a long, lustful kiss.

Softly he ran his hands down her side and along the sensuous curve of her hips. Unbuttoning her dress he let it fall. Moonglow painted the outline of her breasts and the stars bathed them with stardust. Louis traced his finger lightly over their soft fullness, as they rose and fell with every breath.

They kissed again; their bodies pressed tightly together, her heart beating hard against his chest. Each kiss fueled a fire deep within him—a fire that began so long ago in a land far, far, away—a fire that he carried in his heart through suffering and hardship, sorrow and despair—a fire that once flickered, but the spark was kept alive by hope. It now became an all–consuming fire—a fire that melted two souls into one.

Louis picked up Emmeline in his arms and carried her into their house—the house that had waited so long for her—their own little corner of heaven—their Beaubassin.

As he lay her gently down, he whispered, "This is where the sun is shining beyond the storm."

THE END

0-595-21911-X

CPSIA information can be obtained at www.ICGtesting.com
Printed in the USA
LVOW041104260212

270479LV00004B/1/A